MAJOR INQUIRY

'A first-class book that grips you with reality from the first and never lets you go . . .'

Yorkshire Post

'A superior police procedural'

Western Daily Press

'Told with such directness that it grips like an arresting officer'

The Times

MAJOR ENQUIRY

Laurence Henderson

Academy
Chicago
Publishers

Published in 1986 by

Academy Chicago Publishers
425 N. Michigan Avenue
Chicago, Illinois 60611

Library of Congress Cataloging-in-Publication Data

Henderson, Laurence.
    Major enquiry.

    Reprint. Originally published: New York :
St. Martin's Press, 1976.
    I.   Title.
[PR6058.E493M35   1986]   823'.914   85-28718
ISBN 0-89733-199-0 (pbk.)

For
JOE GAUTE

CHAPTER
ONE

The first call was routine. It was made by Mrs Barbara Lewis, the conscientious secretary of the North Road Sports and Social Club, and she called to ask if any accident had been reported involving a sixteen year old girl.

The girl's name was Monica Henekey and she had been last seen by Mrs Lewis at that evening's indoor tennis session. She had left the club at 9.50 p.m. to take the bus to her home a mile and a half away. Mrs Lewis had herself left the club shortly afterwards and she was certain that Monica had accepted a lift from the driver of a passing car instead of waiting for the bus as she said she would.

Mrs Lewis had herself been home for more than half an hour. She lived very near to Monica's home and she had been contacted by Monica's mother who wanted to know why her daughter was so late in reaching home. It was very worrying because the reason that Monica had given for not waiting for Mrs Lewis had been that she had especially wanted to reach home in time to see a particular television programme at 10.15 p.m.

The duty constable made his entry in the occurrence book, noted the time as 10.46 p.m. and pointed out, from the deep wisdom of his own twenty three years, that sixteen year old girls had many reasons for being late in reaching home. They met friends, ambled, got into long conversations, went somewhere for coffee, and simply forgot the time. He told Mrs Lewis that Monica was likely to turn up at any moment and she would be astounded that anyone was worried about her. He made a note of Mrs Lewis's telephone number and checked that there had been no incidents reported in the vicinity of the North Road.

At 11.10 p.m. the girl's mother, Mrs Mary Henekey, telephoned to say that her daughter had still not returned home: all her friends and local relatives had been contacted and none of them had any idea of where she could be. The call was transferred to the duty inspector who recorded the description of the girl—5 feet 2 inches tall, of slim build with long, dark hair held back from the face by a white hairband, green eyes: wearing a white raincoat over a white cotton tennis dress, white socks and tennis shoes: carrying a small purse and also a tennis racquet in a canvas cover. The description was relayed to all area crime cars and foot patrols.

The third call at 11.33 p.m. came from Mr Henekey who had arrived home from the local chapter of the British Legion, where he had attended a committee meeting, to discover his wife frantic at the lack of news of their missing daughter. The inspector sent a policewoman to the Henekey home to compile a list of addresses of friends and others whom the girl could possibly have visited. He also put through a call to the head of the divisional CID at his home, to put him on notice of a possible major enquiry coming up. His nose told him that this one was something more than a young girl being late home from a sports club. He would have been hard put to it to have explained why, but girls who walked about dressed for tennis, with a racquet in their hand, did not fall into the usual category of girls who took two hours to reach home or who were likely to be easily talked into anything.

It even crossed his mind that it might be connected with the series of rapes and killings of girls that had been sweeping the North Eastern suburbs of London during the past ten months, but he did not mention it and neither did Detective Superintendent Graham, whose voice sounded strangely muffled as he instructed the inspector to keep him informed of what happened, either way.

It was not until the inspector put down the phone that he realised that the old man had taken the call in bed and had been speaking without his false teeth.

It was ten minutes past one when he took another call about the girl and it was with a feeling of inevitability that he took it on the Channel 7 handset. The radio call was from one of the crime patrols. Constable Brown had been alone in his Panda car at the far end of Goff's Common, more than five miles west of the tennis club, at the point where the open land of the common merged into Goff's Golf Course. It was a well known area for courting couples and when Constable Brown had first seen a flash of white through the broken hedge at the side of the common, he had made as much noise as possible in opening and shutting the door of his Panda car. He often had to do his own courting in public places and he thought it unfair to jump out unexpectedly on young couples.

When he went through the hedge, his torch showed him the girl immediately; she was lying very close to the hedge, on her back, with her raincoat spread on either side of her like a pair of wings. She was still wearing her tennis dress, the skirt of which had been pulled up to form a neat line across the top of her thighs. There was no obvious sign of injury and her eyes were open.

Constable Brown was very careful not to disturb the position of the girl, or her clothing or any of the ground around her. The body was cold but not icy. Once he had ascertained that she was dead and that no one else was around, he had called up the station and confirmed the night duty inspector's suspicions. After making his call, Constable Brown positioned himself so that he could watch both the body and the road as he waited for the experts to arrive. He switched his torch back to the girl and shone it again on her face, just so that he could see it. He was a young man and the face of Monica Henekey was the most beautiful that he had ever seen.

CHAPTER
TWO

'It will remain cool in the South East,' said the radio voice. 'Mid-day temperatures are expected to be in the region of 50° fahrenheit 10° centigrade. There will be light winds and some rain along the eastern coasts of Kent and Essex but elsewhere it will remain dry although it may become over-cast in places. That is the end of the weather forecast and we now return you to Don Dom and his rhythm time.' There came the booming note of a gong and the first three notes from a strangulated bass guitar.

Arthur Milton flicked the switch of the transistor radio and resumed the leisurely knotting of his tie. He stooped to look at himself in the mirror of the dressing table as he smoothed down the collar of his shirt. He rubbed the spot along the edge of his jaw that always shaved badly. His thin hair had brushed flat against the top of his head, paper flat now that there was no longer any bulk to spring it from his scalp. Although he had had his best night's sleep for weeks, his eyes looked dulled.

He resented his face looking so worn, forty six was hardly old but he seemed to have the sort of face that wore badly: it had seen a lot of living and none of it had been easy.

He flicked down his cuffs, buttoned them and looked at his wrist watch—9.30 a.m. It was a rare luxury to be dressing at such a gentlemanly hour but one that was well deserved. After six solid days on the graveyard shift, he had at last moved into a rest day. And the older he got the more he hated night duty.

He took his jacket from the door of the wardrobe and carried it out of the bedroom and down the stairs to the tiny hall. He went through into the kitchen. His wife had already completed her housework; the plastic top of the little kitchen table shone as brightly as though it had been lacquered. A little bowl of cereal was waiting next to the milk jug.

He brought the teapot from the top of the boiler and shook out the newspaper. The cat had coiled itself up on his chair and regarded him balefully, trying to outstare him. When he put it down on the floor it arched its back and then moved haughtily to the side of the boiler before curling itself up again. Milton glanced only briefly at the headlines of the newspaper before he turned to the sports pages.

The door leading into the garden was slightly ajar and he could see his wife standing at the fence that separated his minute garden from that of his neighbour. His wife was in intense conversation with the woman who lived next door. Milton grinned to himself as he poured the milk over his cereal.

As he picked up the spoon the telephone in the hall started ringing. He cursed and tried to ignore it but it rang on and insistently on. He got up and went out into the hall.

It was Newcombe, the night duty station sergeant. 'Is that you, Arthur?'

'It had better be. What's up, Henry, haven't you got a home to go to? Your tour ended three hours ago.'

'It's like an Irish wedding down here. A local girl's been knocked off. All rest days cancelled, full recall.' He dropped his voice. 'I could mark you as a no reply; they've got more than they know what to do with anyway. The Squad's been brought in, the whole bloody lot of them have turned up all over the place.'

Milton considered; it was very tempting, but then he remembered that his wife thought that it would be a good idea to use the day in having him drive her over to see her sister in Kent. 'No, I'll come in, Henry. I'm having my breakfast first though, I'll be about an hour.'

'The heavy mob's got your old mate in charge, Shenton.'

'He'll be wanting to suck my brains then, just like the old days.'

'Some hopes!' said Newcombe and rang off.

Milton returned to the kitchen but before he reached his chair, his wife came in from the garden. She stumbled at the step, her hair had dropped across her plump face and she was crying.

'Have you hurt yourself?'

'It's terrible, Arthur.'

'What is?'

'Mary Henekey's little girl, Monica. She's been killed, murdered by some . . .' She held the hem of her apron up to her eyes.

'You mean the girl round the corner?' It was a stupid question; snapshots of the girl came into his memory with the speed of light. The toddler who would come into his garden and grab at the flowers before she could talk: the very pretty, dark-haired girl with the sparkling white teeth who smiled when she passed him in the street. 'Little Monica, she won a cup or something, for running.'

'Three years ago. Her poor mother.'

Milton left her sobbing into her apron and went out into the lounge to fetch the whisky bottle. He made her drink some although it made her choke.

'I saw her,' said his wife, 'I can't believe it, only yesterday, when I went . . .'

'Take it easy,' said Milton, letting her cry into his chest. He remembered his wife's interminable knitting and all the bits of her conversation that had washed over him. She had been knitting a shawl and baby clothes for the Henekey's other girl, the elder sister who was heavily pregnant. He thought of the girl's father, Jim Henekey, whom he sometimes saw in his garden; a tall, thin man with a hesitant smile, the poor bastard.

'Newcombe rang just now to tell me, a local girl he said. I'm recalled. He must have known the address, the name. The old bastard tried to put me off.'

'What did you say?'

'Nothing,' said Milton, 'not a thing. Poor Jim and Mary Henekey.'

'Poor all of them, and that poor girl waiting for her baby. I don't know, I don't know why these things happen. What in God's name is it all coming to, all this violence and killing? It was never like this.' She raised her head determinedly. 'I'm going round, if they don't want me then—I might be able to help.'

'It can't do any harm, you do that. I'll get the car out and drop you round there.'

He did not finish his cup of tea, it had been stewed into acid. He lit a cigarette to take the taste of it out of his mouth

and went out into the hall to pick up his car keys. His wife
had only got as far as the bottom of the stairs and she was
crying again.

'To send your daughter off to play tennis,' she said, 'and
the next thing you hear . . .'

He put his arm around her. 'We'll get him.'

'What good will that do her mother?'

'None,' said Milton, 'it never does.'

CHAPTER
THREE

That part of the common on which Monica Henekey had lain was now surrounded by canvas screens. No cars could pass along the road which edged the common because of the road block of police cars and the large caravan that had been towed in to serve as a mobile headquarters. The arc lamps that had lit up the scene throughout the night were still in place but had now been switched off.

Detective Superintendent Graham stood just inside the canvas enclosure, mentally listing, for the umpteenth time, the things that had been done and those that were still to be done. He was very conscious of the man who was standing next to him, Detective Chief Superintendent James Shenton, Commander of the East London Crime Squad, and now the leading investigator into the death of Monica Henekey. Two detective sergeants stood behind them, waiting for someone to tell them what to do. Shenton said nothing and Graham kept his eyes on the ground; the body photographed with close-ups of all salient features, the surrounding area searched by arc lamps, Home Office consultant pathologist brought in to view the body and then to supervise its removal to his laboratory. Forensic examination of the ground beneath the body and then a sheet of polythene pegged down to prevent the collection of dew or to catch any rain that might fall, before it could be examined in the light of day.

Graham turned and nodded to the sergeants. 'We'll have the cover off.'

The two sergeants moved round them, carefully keeping to the extremities of the shelter. They pulled out the pegs and neatly folded back the plastic sheet. When they had finished, Shenton went down on his haunches and peered intently at the formless depression of broken grasses on which Monica had lain.

He leaned forward a little and put up his hand.

'Tweezers.'

The others tensed as he stretched forward and extracted something from within a twist of scrub grass. It was a dirty screw of paper which Shenton had great difficulty in unrolling. The inside had some lurid colouring and then, along its extreme edge a snatch of microscopic print.

Shenton could not be bothered to find his spectacles; he screwed up his left eye to induce myopia and read '——y's (Confectionery) Ltd.'

'Nothing,' he said and dropped it into the envelope that his sergeant held out to him.

He remained on his haunches and looked at the ground again. It was very unpromising; a few square yards of worn grass, the worst sort of ground for retaining anything. A ground that had been trampled over by a thousand feet, lain on by dozens of courting couples, sat on by family picnickers. It had been searched, of course, and would be searched again; the grass cropped, the top of the soil raised and every inch sifted, for anything, anything at all.

Shenton got up from his knees and nodded; Graham took it as his cue.

'The body was taken off before I got the signal, before . . .'

'Quite right, the sooner we have the medical report the better. Who did you use?'

'Camden, he lives this side of London. He came out right away and when he wanted the body moved . . .'

'Couldn't do better than the Professor.'

'He reckoned a report sometime this evening, about nine hours he reckoned for a full autopsy.'

'Thorough,' said Shenton, 'he doesn't take anything for granted.'

Shenton moved out of the canvas shelter and the others followed him in a small procession. He took out his pipe and began to fill it: beyond the shelter he could see the long line of searchers moving slowly across the grass in unison, peering intently at the ground before them. Shenton took his time in surveying the scene, trying to get the feel of his surroundings. Although nothing showed on his face he felt depressed. For ten months now he had had the overall responsibility for directing enquiries into the deaths of five young women who had been raped and murdered in the suburbs that radiated out from North East London. He had been continuously checking and rechecking, evolving plans and planning against contingencies.

For the past four weeks a complicated system of decoys had been in operation. Policewomen had strolled about dressed as dolly birds; imitating typists and shopgirls on their way to and from work. Each of them under the close scrutiny of a special observation squad. On the night of Monica's death, he had had one hundred and twenty men, keyed up and ready to pounce as soon as the bait was taken. But instead of being decoyed by one of his six police-women, a sixteen year old schoolgirl had gone. Sixteen years old, he thought bitterly, the youngest yet and taken in the street.

It was getting out of range, the pattern was breaking up and once that began anything could happen. All the others had been young women, aged between nineteen and twenty six, living in bed-sitters or sharing flats with other girls and all killed there, in their own rooms, raped and strangled. And now this one, a schoolgirl killed on her way home from tennis. It was not in the pattern but that also was likely. To go for something younger, to invite a greater danger; it was probably part of the neurosis, the compulsion of whatever it was called. An academic somewhere would have the right word and all the neat answers, once it was all over.

He finally lit his pipe and watched Graham from the corner of his eye. A prickly man, Mr Graham, and not without cause. Shenton was well aware of the resentment that local officers felt when an investigation was taken out of their hands. I felt the same in my time, he thought, and to be the official head of a CID division who had been raked out of bed in the middle of the night, and put in nine solid hours setting up an investigation, only then to have a Crime Squad wonder boy arrive to take over just when you felt that you were moving into gear, must be galling.

Shenton made a gesture which embraced both the line of searchers and the mobile headquarters. 'You've done ex-tremely well to set all this up in this time, it is very efficient.'

Graham grunted and then looked round as another car came in moving through the road block. He raised his hand in brief acknowledgment to the driver. 'The photographs have arrived.'

'Fine,' said Shenton, 'we'll look at them in the caravan.'

Graham took the large manila folder from the car driver as he came off the grass and then led the way up the two wooden steps of the caravan. Shenton grunted as he followed him, edging his way past the communications equipment and then down the plywood alley into the final compartment. Graham emptied the photographs onto the narrow table and waited for Shenton to take his pick.

They were excellent photographs, full plate and in accurate colour. Shenton examined them thoroughly: the first was of the girl lying as PC Brown had first discovered her, then the perspective shots showing the body in relation to the hedge and the concrete lay-by; then the close-ups, of the legs and neck, the face, hands and body. There were others of the body being moved and then of the ground on which she had lain.

Shenton put them back into sequence and looked again at the first picture, which showed Monica Henekey lying on her back; the raincoat spread to either side of her as if she were an enlarged white butterfly, the legs together and the skirt pulled high.

'And this was how she was found, with the legs together?'

Graham nodded. 'Unusual with a rape, he must have done her somewhere else.'

'Any sign of bruising?'

'I couldn't see any and Camden looked at her nails. He said there was nothing under them, no sign of a struggle or injury. She looked peaceful, as if she was asleep.'

'The tops of her legs?'

'We looked under the skirt, no sign of anything obvious but there was nothing under the skirt, she was naked.'

'And no sign of her underclothes?'

'No sign of anything.'

'Ah.' It was a small sigh. Shenton looked up from the photographs and tamped the top of his pipe down with his thumb. 'You know the man I'm looking for takes the girl's knickers as some kind of souvenir. He's killed five before and is about due for another, so far eleven weeks has been about his limit.'

'But he kills girls in their own rooms, doesn't he?'

'He kills girls in their teens or early twenties. He strangles and rapes them, we're not sure in what order, maybe he does both together. So far he's chosen girls who live in flats or bedsitters and that's where he's done them so far, in their own places, with other people in the same house, sometimes in the next room.'

'He's got the hell of a nerve.'

'Or a kind of madness to increase the tension, the excitement. We don't know how he chooses them, or how he gets them to let him into their rooms. Maybe that's the part that he's finding more difficult. So far as we've been able to check, he never knew the girls, had never even met them before. There's been no kind of common de-nominator at all. All we've been able to do is to wait for him to have another go and hope that we get there in time. I've had six decoy patrols set up for the past month. Maybe he's seen us and decided to try something new.'

'Is there anything at all from the others to show what sort of man we're looking for?'

'A description, you'll have seen that from the handouts. Middle to late twenties, dark hair, well dressed, self-assured. There's nothing else, no accent, physical peculiar-ity, not even a sniff of how he travels, car, public transport or roller skates. According to the psychiatric estimate, the man we're looking for will be compelled to go on until he's stopped or until he stops himself, through suicide. I've heard these stories before and I've seen them proved wrong more often than not. But, for what it's worth, we've been checking on all suicides of men in the right age group. And all that that's told us is that he hasn't knocked himself off. This Henekey girl fits his pattern, if it is him and he's got desperate and killed in his own area, then it could be his first mistake.'

'Well,' said Graham, 'it looked like a local to us. Accord-ing to the woman who was at the tennis club with her, Mrs Lewis, the girl knew the driver of the car who picked her up. I've got my team at the station working out a list, friends, relatives, neighbours, members of that tennis club . . .'

Shenton stretched himself back as far as the wall of the caravan would allow him. 'I had a look at the map in the car but it's not on a big enough scale; this spot is on a continuation of the North Road isn't it, and also beyond the girl's home? Is that right?'

'About three miles, I've got the map here.' Graham brought up his document case from the floor and took out a survey map and spread it across the top of the little table. 'This is scaled three to the mile. The girl's home is here, two and a half miles further back, all those streets turn off from the North Road and two miles further back again is the tennis club. It's almost a straight line from here to the tennis club with the girl's home about half-way between the two.'

'I see.' Shenton traced the route across the map for himself with the tip of his little finger. He continued studying the map as he fiddled about with his pipe, emptying the dottle, restuffing with tobacco and striking matches until he had filled the little cubicle with acrid blue smoke. Graham moved his head away from the thickest clouds and brought out his own cigarettes.

'If he was driving away from the tennis club, keeping to the main road, then this is the logical place for him to end up, it's the first open land coming out of the town. He must have driven at least five miles with the girl in his car and for part of the time she would have been dead. There are no houses around here but it is a main road, and there is quite a bit of traffic, even at night. It's not the logical place for a rapist to take his victim, there are plenty of better places further on.'

'Another mile and you're at Braddon's Wood, twenty feet in from the road there and you're completely hidden.'

'And in a car he could have been there in two or three minutes but he doesn't, he puts her here and the only reason he could have for doing that must be because it was the first possible place. He didn't want her in his car a second longer than he had to.'

'That sounds like panic,' Graham put in. 'If the joker you're looking for, the Beast or whatever they call him, does them with people in the next room, he's not likely to care about carting one around in a car, is he?'

'Not on his home ground. The times he's been seen before, have been by people who can describe him but can't recognise him: if he was seen here it would likely be by someone who could recognise him. It could be by someone who lived in the same street. That could make it very different.'

'If he is a local then we'll have him. He's a lucky bastard to have got this far, picking the girl up on spec, he could have been seen by anybody. It was sheer luck that the Lewis woman didn't see him, there was only seconds in that. He could have been seen on the road, or the girl getting out of the car at wherever it was he took her, and then him having to carry her back to the car, let alone a car passing when he put her out here. There must be someone who saw something and who'll remember when we start pressing. Whoever he is, he's not the Invisible Man.'

Shenton still looked at the map. 'If she ever did get out of the car. She could have been killed in it.'

'That'd be the hell of a chance to take on that road.'

'He doesn't seem to have taken much else.' Shenton raised his eyes from the map and looked dreamily over the bowl of his pipe. 'He put the girl out on this side of the road, the left, which is the same side as he picked her up. That might mean nothing but if he took her beyond this ground and brought her back again then it would be logical to dump her on the other side, otherwise it would have meant him turning his car around in the road once he got her out or carrying her body across the road. I don't see him doing either, because if he was willing to take those sort of chances, he would have dumped her further on in those woods.'

'He could have put her here knowing that we would comb backwards from where he picked the girl up. It's not likely but it is possible, if he's as cunning as you say.'

'It's something to bear in mind but the chances are that it was an impulse killing, that he was on his way to somewhere else and just happened to come across the girl standing on her own on that road. I shall be interested to see Mrs Lewis, but let us accept for the moment that she is right, that the girl did know the driver of the car that picked her up. He hasn't come forward so we have to assume that he was the killer. Now, she couldn't have known that many men, her family, neighbours, boy friends, the fathers or brothers of her schoolfriends and other members of that club. You're making a list, good; were you thinking of anything else?'

'Well,' Graham hesitated for a moment and looked down at another file that he had taken from his document case. 'We've had other incidents around here, attacks on girls and young women, mostly in the area of Greenacre Park which is over in the town centre, close to the railway station. They've been going on for about two years and they look like the work of one man. We've had special watches, extra patrols, the lot, but we haven't got anywhere. He hasn't killed anybody but he has put two into hospital. I thought it possible that he might be branching out, if he was in the mood and the girl was standing there when he came along.' Graham shrugged. 'It comes to the same thing; someone she knew well enough not to have any second thoughts about getting into his car.'

Shenton looked at him without expression but with an interior approval, the thinking was parochial but it was sound, and when he spoke again it was in a warmer tone. 'Whether it's the one I'm after or your man, a local who's gone over the top, the thing is to find him. You've started well with your check on family friends and so on but you can never be too sure about the odd friend of a friend whom no one thinks about.'

He picked up one of Graham's pencils and poised it over the map. 'I think that our man was on his way home. He had no possible way of knowing that he would see the girl standing outside that tennis club. She got in his car because she knew he lived near her and could drop her off without trouble. When he killed her he had to get rid of her body in a hurry and he dumped her in the first open spot, here.' The pencil circled the roads running like a maze between the Henekey home and the North Road. 'That area is, what, an eighth to a quarter of a mile either way. I want blanket cover. Whatever he's done before, an impulse killing is different: he can't be certain that he hasn't made any mistakes, or that nobody noticed anything. It could well have knocked him off balance and if it has we don't want to give him too much time to pull himself together. A full check on every house.' He noted Graham's surprise. 'It's the only certain way, on all the others we've been scratching at nothing; in this one we're going to have information in floods. All but one ten thousandth of it will be useless but that other little bit will be what gets him. The questionnaire can soon be produced.' He grimaced slightly. 'My team have had a lot of practice. You know the man at the town hall who can produce the names, voters' lists and so on?'

'Yes sir, as I said, I've had a full recall of all divisional CID.'

'Fine,' Shenton knocked his pipe out on the aluminium edge of the window. 'Let's go and talk to them.'

CHAPTER
FOUR

When Milton reached the station it was almost mid-morning and his usual parking space, convenient to the back of the station was already occupied by a big Rover. Strange cars were parked all over the place and he had to circle the car park twice before he decided to chance his arm by leaving his car broadside to the wall of the station itself, at an angle which all other drivers would find enjoyably inconvenient.

The corridors were crowded and when he reached the reception area it looked like the end of a football scrum. Leaning against the reception desk were half a dozen unabashed men who looked like national pressmen, and around them stood about twenty recalled beatmen who were waiting for someone to tell them what to do. Milton made his way through them to the CID room and felt a dozen eyes burn into the back of his neck as he opened the door.

An inner pressure held it for a moment and then someone sitting immediately inside moved his seat and allowed Milton to squeeze through. The room was crowded, his own desk had been turned around and pushed against the window to allow a few more chairs to be inserted.

'Get that door shut,' came the peevish tones of Divisional Inspector Durant and Milton had to twist his neck to see that he was sitting at the desk of Detective Constable Sheehan at the far end of the room. Durant had several very large men crowding in at either side of him, all of them were holding files and clipboards. Milton shut the door and all the interested-looking faces that had been turned towards him turned back to whatever they had been looking at before. Everyone seemed to be smoking but no one was saying anything. Sheehan had perched himself on a window ledge, two or three bodies in to the right of the door.

'How's it going?'

'Waiting for the brass, Skip. The heavy mob moved in this morning.'

'Newcombe told me. What are we all crowded in here for?'

'The briefing room's got the Squad in it. The commander took over Mr Graham's room, so he took over Durant's and Durant came out here. Both interview rooms have got the squad circus in them.'

'How long have you been here?'

'I've been at it all night. I went up with Graham and had the lot, putting up screens and searching the lay-by. I went home for a wash-up and was told to go back for a search of the golf course in daylight, but as soon as I got back they told me to come in here. Bloody balls up.'

'Looks like there's going to be a house-to-house then.'

'Not much sense in that, is there? The bloke they're looking for won't be a local, he does them all over, flits about like a blue-arsed fly.'

Milton squeezed himself into the end few inches of the window-sill and managed to accommodate a small part of his behind. It was very restricted: Sheehan was a very large man.

'You knew this bird, didn't you, Skip? Newcombe said she lived next door to you.'

'Next street. My wife's very thick with the mother but I knew the girl all right. It's a damn shame, she was a good kid, one of the best.'

'Johnny Brown found her, he was right cut up about it.'

'They made a mess of her?'

'No, that wouldn't affect him, he used to be on traffic. It was funny, really, he said he couldn't see a mark on her. What shook him was the way she looked. He reckoned she had wonderful looks, never seen anything like her before. That's what shook him, to think that some bastard had destroyed a girl who looked like that.'

'Yes,' said Milton. 'I know what Johnny means. It's the bloody waste of it all, she was a glorious-looking kid.'

'It's a right bastard of a thing to happen to anybody but to a sixteen year old kid—Jesus.'

Milton glanced round the room. 'They've got enough brains here, let's hope they do their stuff.'

'This Chief Super, Mr Shenton—he's supposed to be shit hot isn't he? Newcombe said he used to be on this station.'

'He had Durant's job sixteen years ago. DI under Meadows when he started.' 'A long time ago,' he added, under his breath.

'He's done all right then, hasn't he, DI to Squad Commander in sixteen years. That's some moving.'

'About par for the course, if you're exceptional. If you're like me . . .'

'I didn't mean . . .'

'I'm not sensitive; we can't all be Field Marshals.'

'Is he as good as they say?'

He gave Sheehan a cigarette. 'About the best I've seen and I've seen plenty of good ones. He was the youngest DI they ever had here and you could see how good he was then, it came out of his ears. I'd have laid money on him getting to the top. He's a top jack all right and not only that, he's got some manners. He's a gentleman. If we're not shunted on to the sidelines you could learn a lot from him.'

'Yeah.' Sheehan sucked his cigarette and looked at Milton. To remember working under the commander of a regional crime squad when he was a DI sounded like something out of the Middle Ages to him and Milton had not got anywhere in the meantime. It was a thousand to one against him even making inspector now in the last dregs of his career. Poor old Milton, the willing work horse who was born to be passed over. But then he dismissed the thought; he could have a lot worse than Milton sitting on top of him.

Most of the men who had crowded into the CID room were strangers to Milton. He glimpsed a familiar face here and there and recognised them as men drawn from the bordering divisions, but they were very few, most of them were strangers, and all of them were depressingly young.

Sheehan pushed himself off from the window ledge and raised his hand. Milton looked up to see Christine Wren who had managed to push her way into the room. She was dressed with her usual chic but she looked a little frayed around the eyes.

'Don't say they ordered you in as well.' Sheehan greeted her.

'I didn't mind, I couldn't sleep much anyway.'

'You weren't on duty last night.' said Milton.

'They pulled me out, I was on first call. I had to get a list of friends out of the family.'

'How was it?'

'Pretty hopeless, the father was the worst, we had to get the family doctor in. The mother stood up to it better but she went under about two. They both had to be put under sedation and to make it worse, their other daughter had to be told, she's expecting a baby and that made it very tricky.'

'I know,' said Milton.

'Jesus,' Sheehan drew heavily on his cigarette, 'the poor bastards.'

'How were they when you left them?' Milton asked.

'Dazed, the mother was pulling herself together, she's a pretty remarkable woman. That was about six o'clock this morning, when Mr Graham came, but he couldn't do anything. I mean they weren't ready for it; he told me to phone in what I had to Mr Durant so that he could start a list. He was going back to see them later. I suppose it will be Mr Shenton now.'

'I suppose.'

'It's a bit bloody thick though,' said Sheehan, 'to bring you back here after a night like that.'

She smiled. 'What about you?'

'Well . . .'

The door was opening again and this time the men sitting around it were getting up.

'Here we go,' said Milton.

Shenton did not make a dramatic entrance. He carried no papers or diagrams. He moved slowly through the waiting men, nodding here and there to the faces on which his eye alighted. When he reached the desk behind which Durant was standing he turned and indicated that they should group themselves around him. He waited until they had arranged themselves and then put his pipe in his mouth and struck a leisurely match as he surveyed them.

'I'm sure you all know who I am and those of you who have never seen me before will be able to make a pretty good guess.' He looked mildly surprised at the murmur of laughter. 'Most of you will have worked at some time or another on a major enquiry. For the benefit of those of you who have not I have only two things to say, the first is that any enquiry depends on team work but a major enquiry depends on it a thousand-fold. I happen to be in charge of this enquiry but I am only one member of it and no one man is any more important than another in the long run. A major enquiry is only necessary where it is important to pay great attention to detail and so my second point is the obvious one, that a welter of detail is a very boring thing to have to deal with. But it is the only way to go about this sort of case. It is a detail that will catch the man we want and that detail will be brought to the surface by one of you; it is unlikely that it will be found by me.

'I think I can say since I have reached the position of leading major enquiries, that the essential detail that broke the case was never first brought to light by me, it was an officer in the field, the men making the house-to-house visits, the men checking and cross-checking the statements, men like you. In the course of this investigation you are going to see a lot of people and you are going to see a lot of paper. Ordinary people and ninety-nine point nine per cent of them will be innocent: a lot will be confused, but still innocent. You are going to have to be guided a great deal by your judgment of people, your instincts. Qualities that you have already been using every day since you first became police officers. The man who killed this girl is going to be interviewed, in common with every other man of a likely age in this area. Whether we get him late or early depends on what is noticed about him at the first interview. It is likely that you will interview him when you have already seen a lot of people and taken more statements than you can remember. He will be lying to you and we will have him because you will know that he is lying.

'Nothing special about what he is saying, no one thing that you can pick on, but a feeling. He might be tense because his nerves are on edge. He might get abusive. He might be over-friendly. Anything. It could be simply that you take an instant dislike to him without any valid reason for doing so. Don't be afraid of these feelings. Stick to those impressions that you have. I want them in your report, all of them. Don't be afraid that you might make a fool of yourself.

'You will be provided with a questionnaire which you will complete at each interview, definitely in the presence of each man that you do interview. You do not allow any wife or mother or anyone else to answer for him. And there will always be two of you, every time, no matter how often you have to call back to catch him in. One will ask the questions and the other will be observing, and I mean observing. The observer will complete his own report and attach it to the questionnaire.

'There is some indication that he's young so we are particularly interested in the twenty to thirties age group but the questionnaire is to be completed by every man in the area who is aged between seventeen and sixty. One of the points that the observer will report on is the apparent age of the man's appearance as against his chronological age.

'One more thing, this case will receive a great deal of publicity, a public appeal will also be made. We will therefore be receiving the usual calls and letters but there are always a lot of people who are timid of making an official call. They are shy at being in the limelight or at committing themselves but they could well come forward if they see you in their street. If you are approached do not tell them to call at the station. Pay great attention to them, no matter how rambling, and make sure that you get their name and address. It is the little thing that doesn't seem to be important that nearly always turns out to be very important in the long run.'

CHAPTER
FIVE

Mrs Lewis sat on the edge of the chair that they had given her, clutching a handkerchief tightly to her bosom. She had made an effort with her hair but her eyes were heavily bloodshot and the lines beneath them were darkly purple. Shenton sat opposite her, behind the deal table, but he had placed Graham by the door so that she had to face only one questioner.

'I have read the statement that you made to Mr Graham,' he began. 'It is a very good statement, I only have a very few questions, so that I can be absolutely clear as to what happened.'

Mrs Lewis tightened herself so much that she seemed to shudder, tears started in her eyes again and came down her face to hang unregarded on her chin. Shenton did not move, he did not look away but he made no motion towards her, no vague gesture. He waited with an air of infinite patience and slowly his placidity calmed her.

'In your own time,' he said quietly, 'there is no hurry. We have all day: whatever comes to mind, don't try to pick out what you think is important, just tell me.'

'I . . .,' began Mrs Lewis, 'I . . .'

'How long have you known Monica?'

'Since she was a little girl, she used to come up to the club with her sister, she was only eight or nine then.'

Shenton nodded encouragingly. 'When did you begin giving her special coaching?'

'When she was fourteen: she was a natural athlete, her footwork, timing, co-ordination—completely natural. She was fond of most sports, running, tennis, netball and she was in all the club teams open to her age. She had a beautiful style.'

'She came every Tuesday?'

'Yes, on the indoor court; it is the only night that it is

free. Tuesday evenings, from eight until nine forty-five.'

'How would she get there, was it always by bus?'

'Usually she called for me at my house and we would come along together. When I could I would try to get someone else from the club to come in, a more mature player, to put shots to her; we were concentrating on her backhand. But if there was no one else available, like yesterday, then I would play against her myself.'

'She called for you yesterday?'

'At half past seven, she was always very punctual and we left my home together at about a quarter to eight. We caught the bus at the top of the road and got to the club by about eight o'clock; by the time I had changed and we had put the nets up it would have been about a quarter past.'

'Were there any other visitors, any calls, any interruptions while you were playing?'

'No, none at all, we finished at around half past nine. Then we took the net down, tidied the equipment and I did some book work, I'm the club secretary.'

Shenton nodded. 'What happened when you both came to leave?'

'Usually, almost always, we came back together, on the 9.50 bus, although it was often a few minutes late. The bus stop is outside the club entrance, and the journey only takes seven minutes. Sometimes she would come in with me and have a coffee, we might have one or two points to talk about, and then she would walk to her own home. It's only in the next street.'

'But not this time. Why didn't she leave with you last night?'

'We intended to, I had changed from my tennis clothes, it was about a quarter to ten. I had slightly more correspondence than usual, a particular letter. I was a little late but not very much, perhaps two or three minutes but that would not have mattered as a rule. It had happened before and Monica had waited with me for the next bus, but last night she asked if I minded her going on to catch the first one because there was a television programme she particularly wanted to see and it started at ten fifteen. A programme about a ballet dancer on BBC 2. I told her to go ahead, that I would see her at the stop. If only . . .'

'After Monica left, what happened, exactly?'

'I left myself, not more than a minute after her. I closed and locked the office door and I walked along the path that goes around the building before it joins the path at the main entrance. I could see Monica, that is I could see her through the fence. Our grounds are fenced off by a seven foot wattle fence, it's not very good in some places. You can see through the fence, I mean you can see the outline of people through the weave. She was on the other side of the fence in line with me, at the bus stop, I called to her and then I went off the path, away from her, towards the main gate.'

'Yes,' said Shenton, gently.

'I heard the car come up and then I heard the door close, the car door. I called out, I didn't think that anything was wrong, just that someone we knew was passing and had stopped to offer us a lift. Very soon after, I can't say for sure but just as long as it took me to walk the thirty feet or so to the gate, I reached the road and Monica had gone. I could see the rear of the car a hundred and fifty or two hundred yards up the road, disappearing around the bend.'

'You were surprised?'

'I was very surprised that they had not waited for me. But I took it for granted that she had not heard me call. I did not think that anything was wrong but assumed that she had been given a lift by someone that she knew, her father, or a club member, someone like that. I never dreamt . . .'

'Of course not. What can you remember about the car?'

'It was a big car, I only caught a glimpse as it disappeared round the bend. I only saw the rear, but it was a wide car.'

'What make would you say it was?'

'I don't know, I don't know anything about cars. I don't even drive.'

'What colour?'

There was a long pause and then eventually, but hesitantly, Mrs Lewis said, 'It was a dark colour, not black but a dark colour. I'm sorry but I can't remember more than that.'

'But you can be certain that it was not white?'

'I'm sure it wasn't white.'

'What about scarlet or yellow?'

'I don't think so, I think I would have remembered if it was anything startling.'

'Could it have been grey or blue?'

'I suppose so. I'm just not sure but it was that sort of half-way colour.'

'Is there any possible doubt that Monica did go off in that car?'

'There was nowhere else that she could have gone. I saw her at the bus stop as I left the club house, by the time I had reached the main gate she had gone. It was a minute, less than a minute, the bus had not come up, no other cars had stopped or I would have heard them. She must have left in that car.'

'Do you think that Monica was the sort of girl who'd have accepted a lift from anybody?'

'No, not anybody.'

'Why are you so definite about that?'

'Well, because of the sort of girl that she was. She was popular and very attractive but not really self-confident: she was a retiring sort of girl. She was shy with people that she did not really know, even other members in the club house. I'm sure that she would not have accepted a lift from someone that she did not know.'

'If you are that sure it could be very important. It can only mean that she knew the person who was driving that car.'

Mrs Lewis sat very still. 'Yes,' she said eventually.

'Have you any idea who that person could be?'

'No.'

'Anyone at all, no matter how unlikely: a wild guess?'

'No.' She sat fully upright again and looked Shenton rigidly in the eye. 'I have absolutely no idea at all.'

Shenton waited for some time before he put his next question. 'She wouldn't be shy of taking a lift from some-one she had played tennis with?'

'No, I suppose not.'

'She must have played with quite a number of people in this club. Did she have many boy friends?'

'Not a special one. She used to talk about Jimmy Andrews sometimes, they were at school together and then he left. She told me he was at an adventure school in Scotland. I think he wrote to her.'

'Is there anyone in this club that you think might have done this, Mrs Lewis?'

She looked down. 'How could I accuse anyone of a thing like this?'

'I'm not asking you to accuse anyone but you must know everyone that Monica knew. Is there anyone among them that you would not trust?'

Mrs Lewis was silent.

'We are going to have to talk to everyone, Mrs Lewis. Every single member of this club whether they knew Monica or not. Let me put it this way; is there any member of this club, anyone who would know Monica even slightly, who you would not trust with women?'

'Freddy Dewsbury, but it's inconceivable . . .'

'Why do you think he's untrustworthy?'

'He's a bit—he's always having affairs, but everyone knows that, including Monica. He does not make much of a secret of it. He's involved in a new one every summer.'

'How old is he?'

'About forty.'

'And how old are the women?'

'They vary but they are always married. I've never heard of him being involved with an unmarried girl and certainly no one as young as Monica. But anyway Monica did not even like him, he was such a show off.'

'But she might have taken a lift from him?'

'I suppose—if she was very anxious to get home, she might.'

'That's all I'm asking, that she might.'

'Yes, I'm sorry, I'm being silly.'

'Monica was happy at home?'

'Very happy, her family are very nice people.'

'But she would have had the usual arguments with her parents, the sort that all teenagers have?'

'I don't think so, she was always so cheerful. Monica loved her parents and she was so excited about her sister, she is having a baby. She was a home loving girl, not a—not like . . .'

'No,' said Shenton.

'The person who did this, he's a madman, a monster.'

'But she knew him, you've confirmed that, otherwise she would never have got into his car. There was no struggle, no outcry or you would have heard it. He was someone she knew. Did she know many men?'

'I'm sure she didn't. At least I don't think so, relatives, neighbours, friends but none of them would have—I just don't know.' The tears were coming quickly now.

'Thank you very much for coming to see me, Mrs Lewis, it's been a very great help.' He got up and waited politely for her to get to her feet.

'If anything does occur to you, a name, a detail, it does not matter how trivial, please let me know, however remote or scrappy. Just whatever occurs to you.' He rounded his desk to escort her to the door.

'Yes, I will, of course I will.' He watched her disappear down the corridor towards the stairhead.

'Frederick Dewsbury,' said Graham heavily.

Shenton smiled. 'Just a name. There'll be plenty more before it's over: a list a mile long.'

It was Milton who was selected for a concentrated check on local criminals with convictions for sexual offences.

'Here's the list,' Durant told him, 'all those who are violent with it. You check at the last known address and those who have moved you pass over to the squad. Those you find you pull. Mr Graham wants them waiting for him when he gets back.'

'Back?'

'He's gone to see the pathologist with Mr Shenton.'

'Can I have one of the patrol cars?'

'You can have Sheehan but don't make a meal of it. Mr Graham should be back around six and he wants some action so that means I want half a dozen of the creeps lined up and waiting for him.'

Sheehan was glad to be relieved of the chore of stacking copies of the questionnaire as they came off the duplicating machines.

'It's more like a bloody paper chase than a murder hunt.'

'It's not like the telly,' Milton told him. 'You don't catch jokers like this by charging about in fast cars with the honker going. You have to go where they are, all the way into the poky corners.'

'Corners is bloody right. Have you had a good look at this list, Newbolt and that Potts thing?'

'They're creepy all right, so what they need is a good hard look.'

'What they need,' said Sheehan, 'is a dose of Flit.'

CHAPTER
SIX

Professor Camden was a quietly spoken man who used a low-keyed langauge. He dressed unobtrusively and was of medium height with the remnants of red hair encircling the rim of his head. His ruddy complexion gave him the appearance of a gardener.

As he came in from his laboratory he nodded to Shenton and Graham.

'Certain routine tests will have to be completed on the organs that I have removed. I doubt if they will show anything startling but I must emphasise that anything I say here must be regarded as a preliminary report only.'

'Of course, Professor,' said Shenton and smiled.

The pathologist perched a pair of wire-framed spectacles onto the end of his nose and opened a large notebook.

'She was a perfectly healthy, well-nourished and well-developed young woman. Subject to anything further from the tests, my examination showed every organ to be absolutely normal and healthy, in every way. She did not smoke, drink alcohol or take drugs. There were no obvious signs of assault, stabbing, shooting, bruising, burning or scratching. Absolutely no sign at all. She had a light meal some four hours before she died, comprising of a piece of chicken, some green salad and about half a pint of milk. There was also a trace of chocolate, a very small amount. In my opinion, death occurred sometime between half past ten and midnight. The cause of death was unusual and rather difficult to isolate; it is subject to confirmation but I have no real doubts that death was due to a fracture of the thyroid cartilage. That is the bone immediately before the larynx: it is about the size and frailty of a chicken's wishbone. My assistant will arrange for the photographs and I will have the bone itself suitably preserved because, if anyone should be brought to trial, it will be an essential exhibit.'

'Could it be the result of strangulation?' Shenton asked.

'Definitely not, there was no bruising of the sub-cutaneous layers of the windpipe at all. In my opinion there was a single blow delivered to the exact spot. Whoever did it was either very lucky to hit that spot or he was an expert. It is a known karate blow. Only sufficient force was used to kill the girl and, as I have said, only one blow was struck. If the throat had been gripped manually or by ligature there would certainly have been bruising of the windpipe, and if there had been more than one blow then I would expect to find a more confused fracture of the bone. There were no other marks, scratches or bruises of any kind, the girl did not struggle or fight back. Although she was no great size she was a very healthy girl and obviously athletic. To my mind the blow was delivered frontally but was completely unexpected.'

'Would he have to be a strong man?'

'To be accurate it would not need to be a man at all. I've never heard of a woman killing by karate but it would not require any great strength to have delivered this blow, assuming that the girl was taken by surprise. It would be easier for a man because he would likely be taller and it would have been simply a matter of him raising his arm. I am afraid you cannot absolutely rule out anyone of average physique, man or woman. Given the element of surprise, it is amazingly easy to kill in this way.'

Shenton gave an audible sigh and Camden smiled in sympathy.

'One thing I can tell you with certainty is that whatever the original intention, this did not end as a sex crime. The swab I took was clear of sperm and there is no sign of vaginal entry or any kind of interference. She was *virgo intacta.*'

'What about something less than rape?'

'It's possible but it would have had to have been a very light touch. She was very young, with a clear, light skin which bruises very easily. She was dressed in a raincoat and a white linen tennis dress and all that she had on under that was a white cotton brassiere. She also wore white cotton socks and tennis shoes. The skirt of the tennis dress was pulled up when I saw the body and I presume that that was how she was found. She does not appear to be the sort of girl who would wear nothing under her skirt although that, of course, is something for you to check, but I am pretty sure that she was wearing knickers either shortly after or immediately before her death. There was a line at her waist which could hardly have been caused by anything else. That sort of surface marking fades very quickly, in life it would disappear within minutes. Even immediately after death the elasticity of the skin continues, for a time.'

'Can you narrow the time?'

'It is impossible to be exact but in my opinion, for the sort of mark that I observed to remain to a degree sufficient to be noticeable at the time that I saw the body, means that her knickers were not removed until after she was dead. I would say within seven or eight minutes at the outside and something more than three.'

Shenton made a note. 'So the probability is that he killed her first and took them off afterwards?'

'I would say so.'

'And that's all he does, he doesn't touch her, he even puts her legs together and pulls her skirt down a bit to give her some decorum. That's weird.'

'Unusual.' The pathologist pulled at his waistcoat which had ridden up over his corporation. 'It is certainly different from the other five: it is not a sex crime at all in the normal sense of the word. No one is going to kill a girl just to get possession of her knickers.'

'No,' said Shenton, 'not even in this bent age.'

Camden opened his case again and took out a small plastic envelope. 'The only stain on the girl's clothing was on the back of her raincoat and that was almost certainly a grass stain from the part of the ground on which she was lying. The full forensic tests are still to be completed on her clothing, but I shall be very surprised if anything else comes to light. I have only one exhibit of any interest to you at this stage.' He handed over the envelope. 'This was in the hair at the back of her head, completely embedded in the hair.'

Shenton held the envelope up against the light and shook it gently to rearrange the contents; a short length of finely-linked gold chain moved within. Graham leaned forward to get a better view and Shenton passed the envelope to him.

'She was wearing a gold cross on a chain,' said Graham, 'according to her mother she always wore it. Her grandmother had given it to her.'

'Well, there's a part of it, the rest of it he must have taken with him.'

'Or dropped,' mused Shenton, 'in his car, or wherever, it's possible.'

'I hope he has.' Camden rose to his feet. 'The tests will be completed by lunchtime tomorrow and I shall be able to complete my report.'

'Thank you,' said Shenton and both he and Graham shook the professor's hand.

They walked down the corridor in silence: Shenton was very thoughtful. His head was slightly down and every so often he ejected little puffs of tobacco smoke as he jerked the pipe around in his mouth.

'That wasn't a lot of help,' said Graham eventually.

'I wouldn't say that. This is the first time that he's been put off his stroke. I'm beginning to think that he got the hell of a shock when he found that he had killed that girl.'

'He killed her before he meant to?'

'Something like that. He's not running to form at all, it should mean that he was knocked off balance.'

'What sort of crank is he? That bit about the girl's knickers doesn't make sense.'

Shenton shrugged. 'He took them from all the others, it's his trade mark.'

When Graham returned to the station, Milton had his notes on the known local sex offenders waiting for him. Graham ran his eye down the list and scowled.

'Who says Prickett is dead?'

'Lancashire, sir, they found him two months ago at the back of a Kirby car park and identified him by his prints: alcoholism and exposure.'

'Well, he's no loss: how long has Maltby been out?'

'Six months, sir, paroled into supervised care; he's licensed to one of the Newman Trust, a vicar, the Reverend Spottiswood and lives with him as family at a parsonage in Suffolk.'

'And there's no doubt?'

'None, sir, I've spoken to the locals and they've already checked, apparently they always do if they hear of a nonsense case within a hundred miles. At ten o'clock on Tuesday, Maltby was helping the vicar at a meeting for the handicapped.'

'All right, who did you get?'

'Those three, sir, Potts, Leeman and Slocum. I tried for Jennings but his mother put her oar in, refused to let me through the door.'

'She's worse than he is,' Graham bared his teeth, 'but I suppose the twisted bastard had to be spawned by something. We'll let the squad have her.' He picked up the first of the CRO files and ran his eye down the list of convictions. 'I'll have Potts, where did you put him?'

'The first interview room.' They walked into the room where Potts sat slumped under the eye of a bored constable. Graham sat down at the table, laid the open file out in front of him and took a long, piercing look at Reginald Garston Potts.

Milton sat at the end of the table and took up the pad of interview forms: he uncapped his ballpoint pen and wrote the date and the time, noted the names, including his own, and waited. Graham continued to look at Potts and Potts seemed to become smaller, he sucked in his cheeks and his straggling grey hair fell forward to reveal a large bald crown. He fidgeted and tried to return Graham's glance but Graham outstared him and still said nothing. The longer it went on the less control Potts had over his arms and legs. His eyes flickered anxiously from one side of Graham to the other and fear oozed from him until it almost reached the pitch of a smell. Milton felt the hairs at the back of his neck become erect.

'Are you cold?' asked Graham.

'What?'

'You're shivering.'

'What am I here for?'

'You know, Reggie.'

'No, I don't, I asked Mr Milton and he . . .'

'Come on, you know.'

'I never did it.'

'Did what?'

'I wouldn't do anything like that.'

'You're talking in riddles. What wouldn't you do?'

'I wouldn't do anything like that, to that girl. I wouldn't have killed her.'

'What would you have done to her?'

'I wouldn't do anything.'

'Of course you would, given half a chance you'd do plenty.'

'I never saw her.'

'But if you had seen her, you'd have done something then all right, eh Reg?'

'Please,' said Potts, 'please.'

Graham leaned forward and his voice became confidential. 'What went wrong, did it upset you when you saw her lying there, when you knew she was dead?'

'I didn't, I didn't.' Potts was close to tears. 'I wouldn't do a thing like that; I wouldn't do anything.'

'Wouldn't do anything?' Graham shouted. 'Who the hell did this lot?' He brought his fist down onto the file in front of him.

'Not now,' said Potts, 'not now that I've had treatment, all that's gone—years ago. I wouldn't do anything now.'

'That's what you said last time and the time before that, it's never you and then we prove it is you and you say you are sorry and you cry. Every bloody time. Why don't you cry now, Reggie, is it because we haven't shown you the evidence yet? We will.'

'I didn't do it, I didn't do it. It's not fair.'

'Fair! What do you mean by fair, do you remember the girl in the railway carriage and what you did to her, was that fair?'

'I paid for that, I went to prison. I had treatment.'

'And what about the girl? What treatment did she have, she's not all right, is she, she'll never be all right again.'

Potts sobbed. 'I was home. I went straight home from the dustcart, I never went out. My sister makes me stay in at night. I was home all the time, she's already said, she knows I was there, all night. It's not fair. I've got rights.'

'Don't tell me about your rights.'

There was a long silence which Milton found deeply depressing. He laid down his pen and Graham glanced irritatedly at him. Then Graham stared again at the top of Potts's head before rising abruptly from his chair. 'Get rid of him,' he told Milton as he walked out of the interview room.

'All right,' said Milton.

Potts looked at him in bewilderment. 'You can go,' Milton told him.

Potts took out a filthy handkerchief and wiped his wet face. 'I never did it, I never saw that girl, I haven't done anything, I've had treatment. My sister makes sure that I don't go out. I never did it.'

'Go home.'

'People look at me in the street. They watch me, all the time they look at me. No one speaks to me, only my sister. Everyone looks at me.'

'You go back to your sister: go straight home.'

'Every time something happens, the police come and say I did it. Every time a child is missing or gets hurt, every time, people look at me.'

Milton took him by the shoulder and steered him to the door. At the threshold Potts turned to him and seemed about to say something but then he changed his mind and walked out through the reception area. Everyone looked at him.

CHAPTER
SEVEN

At noon on the second day Shenton stood in the doorway of Monica Henekey's bedroom and gave a shudder of tiredness. Although he had been twenty hours without sleep, he showed few outward signs, the eyes were a little more hooded and the shoulders slumped slightly lower but his demeanour was still that of quiet alertness.

Graham showed greater signs of wear: although, like Shenton, he had shaved and changed his shirt, there were shadows under his eyes and the skin on his cheeks had paled and taken on a taut, shiny look.

Shenton turned in the doorway and glanced back down the stairs to check that the Henekey family had remained downstairs. 'The mother is an exceptional woman.'

Graham nodded. 'The father's a bit of a wash-out.'

'A very exceptional woman.' Shenton turned back into the bedroom, faintly surprised that he had voiced his thoughts about Mary Henekey. It had been a funny thing to say; what he did not tell Graham was that she had vaguely reminded him of a film star that he had been daft about in his youth. But it wasn't only her looks, even in grief a vitality radiated from Mary Henekey like a shot of electricity.

'She backs up Mrs Lewis.'

Shenton grunted, pursuing his own line of thought. 'No one else has been here?'

'Christine Wren had a look round on the night but that's all.'

Shenton sat on the little bed and looked at the room. It was very feminine but in a juvenile way; the paintwork was pink and the curtains over the little window were frilled; most of the space above the bed and dressing table was covered with taped pictures cut from magazines. There was an idealised study of a mare with her foal at the edge of a

lake, several of dogs and horses and at least a dozen of
ballet dancers in full flight. On the dressing table was a
hairbrush backed with an enormous pink silk bow.

He leaned over to open the drawer of the dressing
table—hair ribbons, a comb, some tissues, a jar of cold
cream. A lipstick of subdued colouring, a small phial of
perfume, some pressed flowers, an artificial rose, a rain-
bow-coloured shell. He got up and opened the wardrobe.
The clothes were very simple; three skirts, a jacket, a
couple of dresses, two topcoats. At the bottom of the
wardrobe were four pairs of shoes, a pair of fashion boots,
some slippers and a pair of gym shoes.

Shenton turned to the shelves—handkerchiefs, underclothes, tights, white socks. All clean, all simple and nothing hidden among any of them. He looked under the
mattress, under the bed, turned back the carpet, put his
hand on top of the wardrobe and moved the dressing table
away from the wall.

It was behind the wardrobe that he found what he was
looking for; a chocolate box that was held between the
wardrobe and the wall itself, supported by a small ledge
formed by a strengthening batten at the back of the wardrobe. It was exactly the right height for anyone sitting or
lying on the bed to reach by simply stretching out their
hand.

He emptied the box onto the bed. A collection of ballet
programmes: two snapshots of a boy with determined eyes
who gazed straight at the camera with his arms folded
across his chest. An old exercise book, bulging with inserted scraps of paper: a combination of notebook, diary
and scrapbook. There were attempts at poetry and several
quotations; two from Keats. Under various dates there
were records of where she had gone, the things that she had
done, what she had seen, but most of all what she had felt.
Then there were many pages of undated random thoughts
and Shenton could understand why she had hidden the
book, because the thoughts were intensely private. They
were attempts at expressing emotion, at describing the
beauties of nature but also its sorrows; they expressed a sad
awareness of death and cruelty and the essential tragedy of
life. Monica had been a deeply sensitive girl and there, on

the page, were her innermost thoughts, as finely wrought but also as fragile as thistledown. To read them in the awareness of her death was a moving experience.

Pushed into the back of the book were some loose sheets. They were letters; three in all, from Jimmy Andrews at his adventure school; they were boyish letters although boyish in a serious way; they were signed with his love, but overscrawled as though he was somehow ashamed of saying so and had tried to blur the sentiment. They catalogued what he had been doing, where he had been, various minor feats of endurance. He told her that it would be fun if she were up there and that he was sure that she would like it if she were. Shenton sensed, throwing his mind momentarily into that seventeen year old boy, whose emphasis was on the physical senses and who was less than articulate, even by the standards of his own age group, that they were utterances of great feeling. He missed her and wished she were there. And he sent his love.

He put the letter and the book back into the box, replaced all the other items, and got up.

'Nothing?' asked Graham.

'Nothing.' Shenton got out his pipe and began, slowly, to fill it. 'No names, no furtive love affairs, no older men, no secret life at all. It wasn't that she was backward or unintelligent but she was very sensitive, poetically sensitive; and that made her shy. The old-fashioned word for it is pure. She burned brightly, clean and pure; it was her temperament.'

'But she got into that car of her own free will.'

'That's right, she did, so she must have known him, must have; it's the only thing that makes sense. She got into that car because he was a friend or a relative or someone else, what, a schoolteacher, priest, something like that. Someone she did not think twice about.'

'Or a woman.'

'Yes, maybe, but it's almost certainly a man, as Camden said who the hell has ever heard of a woman killing by karate? But a man, even one who learned it thirty years ago in the army, he'd lash out before he knew what he was doing. And that's how it must have been, instinctive, because however it started, the killing was an act of impulse. If he was trained in unarmed combat he could have killed her in a temper before he knew it.'

Graham wrote 'Check judo clubs' in the open page of his notebook and doodled a circle around it. 'The thing I can't make my mind up about is taking her pants off. Did he take them because he's your joker and that's how he gets his kicks or is he someone else who took them to send us up a blind alley?'

'Ah!' Shenton looked at him with new appreciation. 'I've been thinking about that. It could have been someone who's been reading the papers: he hadn't time to sexually assault the girl but wanted us to link it up with the other killings. On the other hand the world isn't exactly full of people who go around breaking girls' necks. If it was our man then he's the prisoner of this kink of his.'

'Yeah,' said Graham, 'when we get him maybe he'll tell us.'

'If he killed the girl without meaning to he must have been in a right state, whether he has killed before or not, to be driving up a road with a dead girl next to you, passing other cars, houses, that's the hell of a pressure. I've been wondering, if this man's got any kind of family and he has been knocked off balance then he's going to need an excuse: he's probably got a job and couldn't make it.'

'He'd go sick.'

'That's right and if he wanted to make it look good he'd go to a doctor. How many are there in this area?'

'I don't know.'

'There can't be all that many. I'd like to know how many men went to their doctor yesterday or this morning. We can't spend too much time on it but one man who knows the locals, it shouldn't take him more than a couple of days.'

'It's certainly worth a try and I've got the man, Milton, he knows the locals backwards, he's one of them.'

'I thought I saw him, he was CID sergeant in my time here.'

'He still is.' Graham shrugged. 'He's all right but he's slow and bloody bolshie when he gets a bee in his bonnet.'

'He won't have changed then. All right, Milton, have a word with him when we get back to the station, before we see the press.'

'Reporters!'

'They're going to write something anyway, so let's try to see that it's something useful. We'll make it a public appeal and make them think that we feel that they're important. That never does any harm.'

Shenton moved out of the bedroom and onto the landing. Graham picked up the box from the bed as he followed him.

'Do we take this with us?'

'No, we'll give it to her mother on the way out. In time to come she might be glad to have it.'

The newsmen were making a lot of noise as they waited restlessly in the CID room. Durant had pushed three of the desks into a line in an attempt to form some sort of a barrier but two separate television crews had infiltrated at either side and set up camera lights which shone blindingly straight into Shenton's eyes as he took his stand behind the desks. The BBC man, a bland-eyed smoothy with an over articulated tenor voice and the expression of a supercilious camel pushed his hand microphone imperiously forward.

'What I would like to do, gentlemen, is to make a statement which I hope that you and your editors will give the fullest prominence. In the first place, the man that we are looking for is obviously very dangerous. He has killed a young girl and is likely to kill again.'

'It's the Beast, isn't it?'

'I don't deal in nicknames, there is nothing romantic about the man we are looking for. He is a particularly squalid murderer who seeks out the most vulnerable and defenceless victims he can find and then kills them in a callous and cowardly way.'

'But he is the same man who has killed five other girls in North London, isn't that true, come on Chief. Monica was raped and killed in the same way as the others, her clothes were pulled up, weren't they?'

'The medical evidence will be given at the inquest.'

'You've been chasing him for more than a year, and now this one, he's laughing at you, isn't he?' It was a high, grating voice, and Shenton recognised it, Broderick, the screwed-up freelance.

'I cannot comment on that.'

'But you must be aware, Chief Superintendent,' piped the BBC, 'that the public is extremely disturbed and so far your enquiries have hardly met with success. Isn't it true that certain Members of Parliament have made representations to the Home Office about the lack of progress?'

'Every one of my officers is making every possible effort to find this man. They are more concerned than anybody that we have not yet been successful. This man is very cunning, he does not only kill in cold blood but from calculation and makes every effort to cover his tracks, which obviously makes it more difficult to catch him but also makes it even more important that we do catch him. And we certainly will catch him but how and when depends upon the co-operation that we receive.'

'Another petition is being raised for the return of capital punishment. Do you think that the Beast should hang?'

Shenton moved smoothly into evasive gear. 'I do not fix penalties. If anyone has that view he ought to get in touch with his Member of Parliament. What I want to emphasise is that the man who killed Monica Henekey is a local man, he lives here somewhere, he has neighbours, someone lives next door to him or even in the same house. They will have noticed something and perhaps not thought anything of it, an unusual journey or activity, maybe just a noise. It is those people that I hope to reach.'

'Have there been any results from the house-to-house enquiries?'

'We've received a very good response.'

'And a lot of criticism, can you tell us when you expect to get some results?'

'I've already answered that. What we know for a fact is that Monica got into a car outside the North Road Tennis Club at approximately 9.50 p.m. and that the car was then driven in the direction of Goff's Common. I want particularly to appeal to anyone who was in the North Road or who passed Goff's Common, in either direction, between the hours of 9.30 and 10.30, to come forward. I want them to come forward whether they think that they saw something or not. It is very important that we see them in order that they may be eliminated from the enquiry. We require a complete picture of the movements of everyone in the area between those times.'

The main questioners looked sulky but the next question came from a source that Shenton did not know, a stocky man with a tough face and a northern accent. 'Is it true that the girl knew the driver of the car?'

'There are indications that she could have known him.'

'And it's likely that the driver was the killer?'

'We have an open mind on that but he or she certainly has some explaining to do.'

'I'll say.'

CHAPTER
EIGHT

The report of Shenton's press interview was given great prominence by the *Evening News*, which printed in full his public appeal for everyone interviewed during the house-to-house enquiries to co-operate with the best will that they could. He had also appealed for anyone who had driven along the North Road on Tuesday night to come forward, whether they had noticed anything or not, it was important, Shenton had said, for them to be seen so that they could be eliminated from the enquiry.

The staff writers of the *Evening News* had linked the interview with a feature on an inside page in which they recounted the full history of the previous killings, and ended with an opinion from someone's tame psychiatrist about the mental state of the man responsible and the compulsions that would lead a man to rape and murder five girls. He concluded that in the case of Monica Henekey some small detail, possibly a noise, had triggered off his psychosis at the crucial moment.

The newspaper report was read with rapt attention by the man who sat on the edge of the bed. He was barefoot and barechested, wearing only a pair of jeans. He read Shenton's statement but he was much more interested in the feature article. He read it for a second time and then he got up and left the bedroom and padded down the stairs to the carpeted hall. He continued through the hall and into the kitchen and opened one of the drawers built into the sink unit. He extracted a pair of kitchen scissors and, spreading the newspaper across the working surface, carefully cut around the whole of the article. When he had finished, he took the rest of the newspaper and folded it very neatly across its length until it formed a large taper. He ignited one of the rings of the gas cooker and then put one end of the taper into the flame. He held it over the sink as it burned, dropping it into the sink just before the flame reached his fingers. Then he ran water into the sink at full pressure, breaking the flakes into tiny modules of ash: he ran the water out of the sink, poking his finger into the chromium-plated drain to encourage the last of the ash to leave. He then ran the water again and wiped the bowl with a piece of disposable tissue. He nodded once, with satisfaction, and then wiped his hands, replaced the scissors and picked up his piece of newspaper, to return to the bedroom.

Once he had reached the bedroom he closed the door and locked it with a key that he took from the pocket of his jeans. He put the newspaper cutting on the bed and went across to the other side of the room to draw the curtains: only then did he switch on the lamps that were attached to either side of the bed's headboard. In the corner of the room farthest from the bed was a wardrobe standing at a slight angle to the two walls which adjoined behind it. He put out both hands to grasp this by its lower edge, lifted and then swung forward the whole of the wardrobe to reveal a space of some eighteen inches in depth.

From this space he lifted up a large cardboard carton which he carried over to place at the side of the bed. He sat down again on the edge of the bed as he opened up the carton. The first item was a manuscript folder that was bulging with newspaper clippings and he leafed through them, before adding the *Evening News* article to the end of the collection. Next he took from the carton a manuscript book and rifled through the pages, reading an extract here and there until he reached the beginning of the blank pages: he put his hand into the carton again and produced a ball point pen. He wrote down the date and then sucked the end of the pen for some time before he commenced to write. He covered half a page in neatly uniform handwriting.

When he had finished he lay back on the bed and rested the book on his stomach and began to read the other entries: he started at the first page and read steadily. After ten minutes he began to stir but read on, the stirring became more active and sweat began to collect at his hairline; his legs writhed and he tried to control them by closing the thighs tightly together. At the final entry he sat up on the bed, carefully closed the book and laid it down on the floor.

The top of the carton was still open and he put his hands inside and began to remove its contents. A conglomerate collection; several stockings, a chiffon scarf, a torn sweater. Another folder this time of pictures, coloured photographs, magazine pictures; of girls smiling into the camera, posing artfully, with raised thigh or hand spread to conceal the groin. And then other pictures, photographs of girls who did not smile, who had their eyes closed or staring, with their clothes disarrayed; their dresses torn open, skirts wrenched upwards. Their legs spread wide.

The pictures he spread on the floor in a wide circle about the bed and he sat on the edge of the bed to survey them. He took up a black stocking and ran it through his hands before slipping it around his neck and looped it to form a cravat. He plunged his hand into the carton again and came up with a handful of coloured cloth. He separated them in his hands, disentangling the various pairs of girls' knickers. He lay back on the bed and moved them across his upper body and then across his neck and face. He did it several times in increasingly rapid rhythm.

Eventually he put down his hand and unzipped the fly of his jeans and pushed them down his thighs. He lay exposed and moved the knickers down to his groin, using both hands to enclose his penis in bunches of cotton and silk and nylon. As his hands worked he turned on the bed until he was able to look over its edge and survey the pictures that he had spread out across the floor. His breathing quickened until it became that of an animal in distress, an ugly sound of rasping gasps, until with a crescendent sigh he came to his climax.

His eyes dulled and the lids began to close. There came a sharp click from the hall below and immediately the man was awake and tense with eyes as narrowed and aware as a ferret. He rose up and off the bed in a single movement, the knickers and stockings bundled back into the carton. The pictures swiftly collected up from the floor. He froze as the footsteps came towards the stairs.

'Are you in?' asked the woman.

'Yes.'

'I'm making some coffee, shall I bring one up?'

'I'll be down,' he said. He pulled his jeans up from where they had fallen about his ankles and picked up one of the pairs of knickers to wipe the sweat from his face and upper body. Then he repacked the carton properly, carefully replacing the manuscript book and folder of newspaper cuttings at the top. He put the carton back behind the wardrobe and carefully lifted the wardrobe itself back into place. Then he went over to the mirror of the dressing-table and combed his hair. He took a shirt from one of the drawers and pulled it on.

'I've made the coffee,' came the woman's voice again. 'I don't mind bringing it up, if you're still working.'

'No, I'm on my way down.'

'I'll pour it out then.'

'Thanks,' he said, 'thanks, Mum.'

He took one last look at himself in the mirror and a final look about the room; he took the key from his jeans' pocket and cautiously unlocked the door, taking great care to make as little noise as possible. Then he switched off the lights and pulled the door close behind him.

CHAPTER
NINE

Milton began his calls with the doctor whose surgery was closest to the point on the North Road at which the girl had been picked up. Dr Andrew Buchanan LRCP MRCS had a very active practice and Milton had to wait for almost two hours until the morning's coughs and sneezes had been given their attention before he was able to go in. Buchanan was Milton's idea of what a family doctor should be: he was about sixty with sparse white hair and bushy eyebrows which shot out like an outcropping above the little shrewd eyes. He listened intently as Milton said his piece and then he leaned back in his chair and put the tips of his fingers together. He spent some more time looking at the ceiling before he returned his gaze downwards again.

'A patient's record is confidential.'

'I know that, doctor.'

'What would happen if I refused to give you this information?'

'I don't know,' said Milton truthfully. 'I would have to report back to my superiors. I imagine Mr Shenton could obtain an order of some kind if he thought it was important. I'm not saying he would. At this stage it is a matter of requesting co-operation: that is as far as my brief goes.'

'If it was a matter of gunshot wounds, or a wound of any kind, scratches for example, there would be no question of not passing the information to you, but any man who consulted me on Wednesday? I can't see the point of that.'

'I believe, that is, Mr Shenton believes, that the man we are looking for is likely to have consulted a doctor. We do not know but it is a strong possibility. It is something that should be checked.'

'What exactly are you looking for?'

'We believe that what this man did on Tuesday night had a tremendous effect on him: that it's possible that he was still in a state of shock the following day. He would have needed to have had an excuse for being in that state and the logical thing would have been for him to say that he had something wrong with his head, or back or stomach. If he had a family it is likely that they would have insisted on him consulting a doctor, particularly if it was unusual for him to be unwell.'

'What you really want, then, is anyone complaining of anything where there is nothing obviously wrong but which could be an emotional upset. The sort of people who come in because they're having rows with their wives, and then complain that they've got a stomach ache.'

'If you have them listed.'

'Oh, I have them listed all right.' Buchanan got up and went out to his receptionist; he returned with an enormous desk diary. 'One of the delights of operating under a bureaucracy is that everything has to be listed, in triplicate. What date was that again?'

'Wednesday and Thurday, the 19th and 20th.'

'Very well,' Buchanan turned the page. 'Caldwell, Kater, Martin, the addresses will be on their health cards. I'm only glad that you don't want the women who come in with their aches and pains.'

'Males only, between seventeen and sixty.'

'You'd better put this one down as well, Mrs Purvis. She came to see me for her husband, she said he insisted on going to work but he was sleeping badly and was depressed. She thought it was something to do with his job.'

'What did you say?'

'I said that he must come to see me himself.'

'And has he?'

'No.' Buchanan waited until Milton had completed the note and then turned the next page of the diary. 'Ready for the next lot?'

At the end Milton had nine names and addresses in his notebook: he recapped his ball point pen and flexed his wrist.

'You've been very helpful, doctor, thank you.'

'How helpful, I wonder.'

'Very.'

'You'll see these people, question them. How will you

know if any of them did it. You may see him and not know.'

'Perhaps not.'

'You're experienced, of course, you must be. But, if he's in control of himself, and cunning, he's not likely to give much away. It could all be a waste of time.'

'Every profession has its failures, we certainly have more than enough in ours. It doesn't stop us trying the next time, any more than it would you or any other doctor.'

'You surprise me, Mr Milton.'

'Sir?'

'That you're only a sergeant.'

Shenton did not arrive at the station until almost eleven on the third day of the investigation: he had been conferring with other of his officers in the Crime Squad who were still deployed in their original areas, patiently watching and waiting for any reaction to the decoy policewomen who still walked the streets and sat in bed-sitters waiting to be attacked. He had also had to make his report to the National Controller of Crime Squads, who was perturbed at the manpower being expended with so little apparent return.

It had all been necessary but it had also been dull and very tiring. Shenton did not have the great natural talents of a civil servant because he found the whole rigmarole of departmental justification and corner jumping to be very tedious. It was a relief to return to the action.

Graham had been waiting for him.

'A couple of things have come up. The uncle was seen as part of the routine check: I've got the report here and he's going to need a good, hard look. But before that, you remember the tennis club Casanova that Lewis woman told us about.'

'Dewsbury,' said Shenton, 'Frederick Dewsbury.'

'That's him, he was seen on the house-to-house as well and made a statement.' Graham produced the sheet from his folder.

'He lives on the North Road itself, very close to the bus stop that the girl usually got off at to walk down to her home. He's forty two, married and a qualified electrical engineer. His car is a Vauxhall 101E. The statement he

made was in the presence of his wife and he said he was out
from eight until around eleven o'clock working in a Scout
Hall in Ridley Road, which is the other side of the North
Road. He's a member of the Ridley Road Amateur Dramatic Club and he went over there to work on a lighting
circuit for a play they were going to put on. He said his
witness was an Alfred Jarrett who helped him out on the
wiring. He was very vague about the times. His wife was in
bed when he got back and she said she went up around
10.45.'

'And what does Jarrett say?'

'Dewsbury was a bit unlucky there because Jarrett had
already been seen. He says that Dewsbury did come up to
the hall but went off well before nine, after he'd drawn up
the wiring lay-out. He left Jarrett to do the actual wiring
because, he said, he'd had to bring some work home, an
important job that he had to finish before the morning.
Jarrett himself worked on for another half hour and then
went home. His house is nowhere near the North Road and
his wife confirmed that he got there well before ten.'

'Interesting.'

'It gets better. Dewsbury rang Jarrett and found what a
hole he was in. He came up here last night, asking for the
officer in charge. Coughlin saw him.'

Shenton propped both elbows onto his desk and cradled
the bowl of his pipe in the palms of his hands. 'How did
Coughlin handle him?'

'Took his statement and told him that we'd need to see
him again. This second statement is a right load of mooley.
He says he got bored with working in the scout hut, once
he'd solved the circuit problem. He decided to leave Jarrett
to it and call on a friend of his called Harold Tine, for a
drink and a chat. Tine lives fifteen miles north and Dewsbury says he drove there, right up to the house. But, he
says, it wasn't until he'd reached the house that he remembered that Tine was still abroad for his firm, so he decided
not to bother Mrs Tine but to drive back home. He took a
long time to do that because he went right out of his way to
avoid the main roads, he says he likes driving up country
lanes, and he says he did because he didn't want to get
home any earlier, his wife always wanted to watch tele-

vision and that bored him. So, he thought it was better to stay out until she was in bed, otherwise he would have got irritated and they would have had a row. I bet they have a lot of rows.'

'Where is he now?'

'At work. I've rung him and told him to be here at six and the cheeky bastard tried to argue. I put the fear of Christ up him.'

Shenton grinned. 'I bet.'

'I told him that if he was one minute late I'd have a squad car round his house to pick him up.'

'I think we can expect him. Milton mentioned the uncle to me; has he come up with anything?'

'Milton's still going round the doctors. Field saw the uncle as a preliminary check on the list of relatives. He was due to be seen, anyway, lives in the check area about six streets from the girl. Field wasn't impressed: he's put in a special report.'

'Is that it?'

Graham passed it over and Shenton put it squarely in front of him on the desk and then put a fist on either side of his face as he commenced to read.

Henekey, Edward. Aged 31. Carpenter, married, two children ages two and five. Address: 18 Maroon Street (Council Estate). Younger brother of Monica's father. Uncle of murdered girl. Car Owner: 1965 Ford Prefect: colour Dark Green: dilapidated condition.

Not frequent visitor to girl's home but all members of both families know each other.

Attitude to questioning: sullen and resentful. Does not appear to be upset at his niece's death. Wife present during interview but timid and unforthcoming; appears to be frightened of husband.

Edward Henekey stated: 'Car broke down on Monday 18th, spent Monday and part of Tuesday working on car to make it roadworthy. Caught cold working in garage and decided to take rest of week off.' On evening of 19th stated, 'Car running but kept stalling, adjusted carburettor and took it for a run. Wanted to get out of the house. I had not been out since Saturday: youngest son crying, wife complaining. Got fed up. Drove around, had a drink in Cricketers at edge of Toms Park, left about ten. May have come up the North Road, cannot remember.'

No corroboration. Not remembered at Cricketer's Public House. Wife in bed on return.

Note: 1. Edward Henekey has poor employment record. Changes jobs frequently amongst a number of building contractors. Rarely retains position longer than 3 months. Frequently in receipt of Social Security benefit. Is regarded as shiftless.

2. Physically capable although no known specialised knowledge of karate or unarmed combat. Height 5 feet 10 inches. Medium build.

3. Edward Henekey has been previously convicted of the following offences.

i) Theft of copper wire.
ii) Theft of articles subject to Hire Purchase Agreements.
iii) Theft of Motor Tax Certificate.
iv) Four motoring offences (one charge sheet)
CRO Reference 897647/1964

'He would have had time', said Shenton.

'And he's in the family. They didn't like him, I don't suppose the girl liked him, but he was family and if he came along that road at the right time and stopped, she'd have got in. What else would she have done, turned him down? She would have been too polite for that.'

Shenton puffed a perfect smoke ring that hung lazily in front of him for a half second. 'Any other reason?'

'He fits the bill. He's a nasty piece of work who's bored with his wife. He was in a lousy temper and he's the type who hates anything better than himself.'

'I agree.'

'Shall we have him in?'

'I don't think so. If it is him he'll be the better for sweating, but he should be watched.'

'I've asked for observations, all sightings to be logged, where he is, what he's up to, but not a full watch.'

'Have him put on a twenty four hour watch for, what, a

week, and check if he goes to the inquest or funeral and of course, if he goes near the Henekey house, but he's not likely to do that.'

'And if there's nothing in a week, we see him?'

'The wife, I think, first.'

Milton rose from his hunched position over the CID typewriter and stretched his shoulders back as far as he could to ease the rick in the back of his neck. He was pleased with himself: his list had grown to fifty one names, all of which he had painstakingly typed out with addresses and subsidiary comments and, as he could only type with two fingers, it had taken him a long time. He shuffled the pages neatly together and carried them down to the end of the CID room to Durant.

'All right, get it entered into the murder log,' said Durant in his purse-lipped way, 'then four photocopies and they all need cross-referencing with the house interviews. Take it up to Charles yourself and make sure he knows that it's top priority.'

Sergeant Charles was an extraordinary figure to find amongst the bright-eyed young members of a crime squad. He wore an elegant, if old-fashioned grey suit, and with his abundant white hair and ravaged profile he had the air of an old-style diplomat.

When Milton laid the list before him, Charles popped a pair of kidney shaped glasses down to the end of his nose and looked at him over the rims. 'Already? I'd have thought you could have strung this lot out for a week.'

'Most of them are in group practices. I'll have finished the lot tomorrow, with any luck.'

'You won't get any pats on the back for that,' said Charles, 'it's the rest of us who'll get a kick up the arse for not keeping up.'

'It's usually the other way round.'

Charles raised an ironic eyebrow and negligently flipped the list into a filing tray on the long table, at which two police cadets sat studiously writing up card indices. 'They're the boys to get it sorted, all young, keen and raring to go: it's a pity they have to grow up and be corrupted.'

'Do you corrupt them?'

Charles grinned. 'I do my best.'

Milton left and went up the stairs to the canteen. Old Lil had gone home and the only coffee available was from the vending machine which was playing up as usual. He had to kick the hell out of it to get anything for his money, and even then, the milk lever did not work.

Newcombe was sitting at one of the little plastic tables, looking as gloomy as anyone who was waiting for night duty to start was entitled to. Milton went across and gave him a cigarette.

'I've been chatting to that collator bloke, Charles, funny to find someone like him in a squad circus. He looks like something out of the 'thirties.'

'He's not that old, got about another five to do.'

'You know him?'

'Used to, about fifteen years ago. I was on the beat then, over the other side of the river. Charles was the CID sergeant, very bright, broke all records, got made up at what, twenty five or six. But he got a bit too bright, especially with women; he got mixed up with some slag, a band singer, which was messy anyway because he was married at the time but the real trouble was that she was married as well: to a right tearaway who was doing ten years.'

'And that was the end of Charlie boy.'

'I don't know why he didn't get out, I would. But he doesn't miss much, he knows his game. If he didn't Shenton wouldn't use him.'

Milton got out his notebook. 'Remember Tommy Skeating? I've got his name down for a special check, lives in Maddern Lane, warehouseman, but he's the footballer, isn't he?'

'Yeah, that's him. I saw him play for England—six— seven years ago against France. It wasn't much of a game but Tommy did all right; fast and lots of guts, a great crowd pleaser.'

'He's only twenty seven now!'

'He got a broken leg and his cartilages went. It was the hell of a pity because he wasn't a clever player, no ball artist. He was a strong boy who could take a lot of stick and stay on the ball. He was all right when he was with the

Spurs, in those days they had a lot of ball players, all teeing it up for him in the goal area. He scored plenty.'

'Until his knees went.'

Newcombe shrugged. 'It's all happened before, a drop into the Second Division, then the Third, got knocked about and into fights, then banned and out of the league altogether. It just happened quicker to him than it does to most.'

'Would you say he was bitter?'

'He's entitled to be: it's only six years since he had it all, foreign tours, interviews on the box, big money, big cars and the cheers of thousands and, suddenly, whammo, and it's all over. Wouldn't you be bitter?'

'Has he ever been in trouble?'

'Drunk a couple of times, never any trouble.'

'Nothing else?'

'He's not your bloke, Arthur.'

'How do you know?'

'Because he's never been short of it. He might have come a long way from the top but he's still got his wife, a beauty queen from somewhere and she's still got her looks. This warehouse job up at the shirt factory really means that he runs the firm's football team. That place employs a lot of girls, he's surrounded by nooky all day. If he wanted it he wouldn't have any trouble at all. He just wouldn't need to pull a bird in the street.'

'OK,' said Milton, 'so you've convinced me but he'll still need seeing, for the system.'

CHAPTER
TEN

Mr Frederick Dewsbury called at the station at a quarter to six o'clock and asked to see the officer in charge. He was accompanied by a slim blonde who peered at everything with great interest through very wide blue eyes, and smiled very prettily at Newcombe when he asked them both to take a seat on the far wall, by the rubber plant.

The smile was lost on Newcombe but not on PC Bell who was also behind the desk.

'That is one very fair piece of crumpet, what's she been up to?'

'All of it by the look of her. The bloke is booked down for Mr Graham as soon as he's free. Where is he?'

'Up with Mr Shenton.'

'Well, keep an eye out for him.'

Dewsbury and his friend had to wait well past six o'clock before any further notice was taken of him. He twice approached the desk and asked if they were sure that Mr Graham was aware that he was in the station. He did not mind waiting but he did not want there to be any misunderstanding about the fact that he had arrived and would not therefore require any transport to be sent for him. He did not want anyone to waste their time.

At twenty minutes past six Graham rang the desk and told Newcombe to have Dewsbury brought up to Mr Shenton's room. PC Bell was delighted to oblige and took them along the corridor. When they reached the stairs he courteously stepped back to allow them to precede him and then followed, his nose level to the hem of the girl's skirt.

Graham and Shenton both stood as they came in and neither showed any surprise at the presence of the girl. Graham came round the desk to push an extra chair forward for her.

Dewsbury held out his hand. 'Dewsbury, Fred Dewsbury, I've come along to clear up this little misunderstanding.'

'Sit down,' said Shenton, 'I am Detective Chief Superintendent Shenton and the gentleman on my left is Detective Superintendent Graham. And what is your name?' he said to the girl.

'Lane, Beverley Lane.'

'Miss or Mrs?'

'Mrs.'

'So now we know who we are. I have reason to believe, Mr Dewsbury, that you have told quite a number of lies to several of my police officers. Apart from why a man should tell lies to policemen, particularly when it concerns a murder investigation, I am going to tell you now that I want to hear the truth. You are going to tell me where you were on Tuesday night and exactly what you were doing. Everything you say will be taken down and you will sign it. Every fact in your statement will be checked and if you lie you will find the consequences extremely unpleasant.'

'Right. That's why I'm here, to clear it all up. I don't like telling lies but I had to, it was awkward. I couldn't do anything else.'

'You admit then,' said Graham, 'that the statement you made to the officers who called at your house and the statement that you made to Chief Inspector Coughlin in this station last night were both false?'

'Yes,' said Dewsbury cheerfully, 'both of them, a complete load of old mooley. I mean, I had no option, my wife was sitting there wasn't she, listening to every word. I couldn't say anything different to what I'd already told her, and then when I rang up old Jarrett and found you'd got me by the short hairs, I had to do something, didn't I, to hold your hounds off till I got it straightened out. I had nightmares of you coming round to rake me out of bed once old Jarrett dropped me in it.'

'Or until you could fix up another alibi which was another pack of lies.'

'Oh no,' said Dewsbury with great earnestness, 'nothing like that. But I had to talk to Beverley first, otherwise she would have been dropped in it as well, not knowing what it was all about. And you would have called on her, wouldn't you, at her house?'

'And we won't now?'

'Course not, look, I'm sorry about all the trouble I've caused. Truly sorry, I panicked. I just didn't know what to do. The truth is that Bev and me, we've been friendly for six or seven months now. And that's, well, I suppose you can guess, we're both married and naturally we have to keep everything dark.'

'Naturally,' said Beverley.

Graham put his fist on the desk. 'Where were you on Tuesday night?'

'I've told you, I was . . .'

'From the beginning,' said Shenton.

Dewsbury dropped his lip, like a sulky boy. 'I went up to the drill hall like I said before, I was there half an hour, working on the lay-out of the circuit. I left Jarrett to get on with it, then I drove round to Clarendon Gardens.'

'Where's that?' asked Shenton.

'It comes off the North Road. I left my car at the top of the road and walked down the lane opposite, it's a foot-path. Beverley, that is Mrs Lane's house is in the road that runs parallel to it, the end of the gardens come out into the lane. I went in through the back gate, the one at the end of the garden.'

'One moment,' said Shenton, 'how did you know it was safe to do that? Were you expected?'

'Oh yes,' said Beverley, 'I phoned him at work. I told him my husband had gone up North and that I was on my own. I told him that the gate would be unlocked.'

'Go on.'

'That's it, I went in and stayed there, all the time, until I came out the same way; picked up my car and drove home. I got home about half eleven.'

'What time did you leave?'

'About ten or quarter past eleven. About that.'

'How do you know, did you look at your watch?'

'Well, no, not when I left. I looked at it earlier and saw it was almost eleven and I said I had to get home. I couldn't be too late. By the time I left it would have been about a quarter of an hour after that.'

Shenton turned to the woman. 'Did you look at the time?'

'Well, I don't think so, but it was about the time that Freddy says.'

'When you noticed the time,' said Graham, 'you were in bed?'

'Well, yes.'

'How long had you been there?'

'Look—I came here of my own free will.'

'After you'd already given two lying statements. And now you're trying to prove that you didn't commit murder. How long were you in that bed?'

'From when I arrived.'

'All the time?' Graham was looking at the girl.

'Yes,' she said, 'that's right. After I'd let Fred in through the kitchen and locked the door we went straight upstairs to bed. We stayed there until he went home.'

'Does this happen every time?'

'Not always but we generally end up, I mean . . .'

'Why,' said Shenton, 'are you both so certain that it was on Tuesday night?'

Beverley gave him a bright smile. 'Because George had gone North. He always goes up on a Tuesday night, it's his usual sales trip, then he comes back late on Wednesday; that way he's only away one night.'

'He doesn't like being away from home?'

'Of course not, he hates it.'

'And how long have you and Mr Dewsbury been whiling away those Tuesday evenings?'

'Oh, five, no, almost six months now. Since about a week or so after I joined the drama group. That's right, isn't it Freddy?'

Dewsbury nodded sourly.

Shenton kept his face completely under control and merely looked at Graham whose brows were knitted at their most ferocious.

'So what it comes to,' Graham began, boring his gaze straight into Dewsbury's left eye, 'is that when you'd got out of bed and dressed you drove back up the North Road. You know Monica Henekey, so when you saw her at the bus stop, you wouldn't be able to resist pulling in to play the big man, would you?'

'No, no, of course not, how could I? I'd just been . . .'

'But that wouldn't make any difference, would it?' Graham continued cruelly. 'It would whet your appetite, particularly a girl of sixteen—make you feel as though you were young again. We know you're famous for that, can't resist chancing your arm with anything, you like to have four or five on the go at the same time, it makes you feel like a big man. Makes you feel important. But Monica wouldn't take a pass from you, she'd struggle, scream. She'd have ruined you if she'd told your wife, not that your wife doesn't know all about you, but to be turned down by a kid. To be known as a cradle snatcher, to be made ridiculous. You couldn't stand that.'

'I didn't, I didn't. God, I never saw her. I went straight home. I swear to God I never touched her, never saw her.' Dewsbury had tears in his eyes but whether from fear or vexation it was impossible to tell. All three were looking at him now and a long silence filled the room. Dewsbury stared blindly forward and Beverley Lane turned her eyes from him and lowered them to look demurely at her hands folded in her lap.

'All right,' said Shenton eventually and picked up the phone. 'I'll have you taken to one of the interview rooms and the officer there will take a statement from each of you. You will then sign it and then be free to go. We may need to see you again. If so, you will be notified.'

It was PC Bell again who arrived to take them down, this time with instructions to deliver them to Chief Inspector Coughlin.

'Coughlin will rub his nose in it,' said Shenton, 'after being had on a bit of string, last night.'

'It wasn't all kidding,' said Graham. 'I still say it could be him. He's the type.'

Shenton shook his head. 'Monica was picked up before ten. By the time Dewsbury left that house, she was already dead.'

'They could have been lying about the times. No, I suppose not that much. But what a bastard, eh? What a bastard, he creeps round there every Tuesday night, and leaps into the other bloke's bed, every bloody Tuesday, like a timetable.'

'It happens,' Shenton interposed mildly. 'Everywhere and any time and it always takes two to make it happen. He's a ram but he's soft: he only goes where he's welcome. We're looking for a very different character.'

'He's off the possibles then?'

'Definitely. He's wasted a bit of time but I wouldn't mind a few more stories like that. It would cut the list down.'

CHAPTER
ELEVEN

The last doctor on Milton's list was his own. He hardly ever visited a doctor himself but he knew this one quite well because of the many visits made by his wife for her mysterious backaches. Dr Godfrey was a very well-built man who had once played rugby to a good club standard. When Milton went in he had pushed back his chair from the old roll-top desk and was gazing with weary boredom out of a window which looked onto an ill-kempt garden.

'Don't jump,' said Milton, 'we'll go together.'

'It wouldn't be far enough,' said Godfrey, 'to kill a tough old bird like you.' He stayed at the window while Milton sat himself in the patient's chair. 'What's this in honour of, or has all that second rate beer finally caught up with you?'

'I've come to ask you something professionally.'

'Whose profession, yours or mine?'

'Mine.'

'That sounds interesting.' Godfrey came back to the desk and opened a drawer to take out an ashtray and packet of cigarettes.

'Don't you believe those posters out there in your waiting room?'

'I believe them all right,' Godfrey lit up. 'The trouble is that I'm a drug addict. I've already had your friends call on me, you know, but I'm hardly a minnow in your net. I live miles away.'

'I know,' said Milton, 'you live in Broad Walk with all the other rich crooks. What I'm after is the names of the men in the right age group who needed attention on the 19th and 20th, particularly anyone who could have been emotionally upset.'

'Really,' Godfrey came forward in his chair, 'you think this man had to see a doctor?'

'It's a fair bet, we think he might have needed a bit of

time to pull himself together and had to have an excuse, a headache, bilious attack; something like that.'

'What a cunning lot of bastards you are.'

'We have to be,' said Milton defensively.

'I'm not complaining, I'm lost in admiration although I could tell you to take a running jump.'

'You could.'

'Has anyone done that?'

'Not after I explained that all the men would be seen anyway and that all we were asking for was an indication that could mean that the innocent ones could be disturbed as little as possible.'

'He needn't have gone to a doctor, you know, a lot of people take a day off and never see anybody.'

'It's very much on the off chance, but it is worth checking. Anything is worth checking on a case like this.'

'All right, let's have a look.' He turned back the pages of his desk diary and slewed the book round at right angles so that Milton could just read the page. Godfrey ran his finger down the page. 'Hello,' he said, 'I'd forgotten about him.'

'Green, you mean Jerry Green?'

'That's him, I'd forgotten completely, but he didn't come in; his mother rang up later and said it was his usual thing but his head was so bad and she was too busy to get out of the house, and could I put out a prescription for her to collect.'

'Well, that's one for his nob, he's on the list anyway, with his record.'

'You can forget him,' said Godfrey. 'If he'd laid a finger on that girl he would have been standing next to her when she was found. There would have been marks all over her and he would have been in an institution by now. Even if he had made it to his home in some way his mother would have called you.'

'She *is* his mother!'

'And a damn good one. I have the utmost respect for Mrs Green. If she hadn't been his mother he'd have spent the last twenty years in a closed institution. She's cared for him, watched over him, ministered to him all her life. She's sacrificed her own life trying to do the best she could for him. But she is a woman of absolute principle and if she thought he was dangerous to anyone at all, let alone a young girl, she would have him put away. I've no doubts whatsoever on that. She is a lady of great integrity.'

'You've thought about this before?'

'Of course I've thought about it. It's natural to think about it when I've got a patient like Jerry Green on my books. If I didn't think that Mrs Green could control him I'd have had him put away myself. She never, absolutely never, lets him out at night. Why don't you check?'

'They'll have done that already.'

'If he was out that night they would have had him up at your station, wouldn't they?'

'Yes,' said Milton, 'but she is his mother, isn't she, and it would only be her word that he was home.'

'And she wouldn't lie. If there's any doubt about that then they can see me.'

'I'll tell them but I agree with you. I can't see Monica letting him get within spitting distance. Right, I've put him down, who else?'

'Only one more man, it was a woman and babies day. Carmichael was the other one, he broke his leg three weeks ago and he came up here on crutches, so you can forget him as well.'

'You've missed one, the last name, Mr LeRoy.'

'Oh, that was just to remind me. He didn't come here, I went to see him, I took a prescription up to him.'

'You don't usually do that.'

'It was on my rounds, as I went home to lunch. He lives a few houses away from me in Broad Walk. It was an urgent prescription, he rang me and he wanted it for that day.'

'What was wrong with him?'

'Look, Arthur, enough's enough, I've done what you wanted. I told you who called, I don't have to give you a history of every one of my patients.'

'But I'm not asking you for that, just men who received treatment on the day after a girl was murdered. Who the hell is LeRoy? Don't you think private patients count, or something?'

'I am telling you that LeRoy doesn't come into the orbit of what we've been talking about.'

'Why not, is he bedridden? Is he a cripple?'

'You know, Arthur, you can be a very aggravating man.'

'I'm used to being told that. It happens every time I refuse to be put off: when I insist on doing my job.'

'LeRoy's illness is a matter of confidence between him and me as his physician. I am telling you that his illness has nothing to do with Monica Henekey.'

'And I believe you. I don't know how we got into this argument. All I've been told to do is to make a list of men who called for their doctors on a certain couple of days. No one wants to pry into their personal lives without cause; no one is going to embarrass them. But I write down a name and you practically bite my head off.'

'I'm sorry, Arthur, forget it. I just had the thought of a policeman calling on the poor devil.'

'It wouldn't be done just like that, but even if it was, why so coy? Policemen are knocking on doors all over this town. I'm sorry but I can't just forget it. I've got his name and it will have to go on the list. If someone decides he's to be called on then he's called on. I can't do anything about that.'

Godfrey glared at him and then closed his eyes and sat back in his chair. Milton waited and when Godfrey opened his eyes again, he was calmer.

'All right,' he lit another cigarette. 'Danny LeRoy has malignant carcinoma of the lower intestine. It will shortly affect not only the whole of the stomach and genitals, but also the base of the spine and it is inoperable. He is aware of his condition and it is his wish that it should be kept from his wife for as long as possible. The condition is worsening and he is in frequent pain and requires morphine, which I prescribe. On the 19th he was in agony and I took the drug to him. I keep a small supply specifically for him, he does not intend to commit suicide but he does not want the drug or syringe in his house in case it arouses his wife's suspicions. She believes that he has a stomach ulcer which causes him spasms. I have given him my word that I will not tell her until the end.'

Milton sat very still. 'The poor bastard.'

'Yes,' said Godfrey, 'The poor bastard.'

'It's usually the other way around, isn't it? The relatives knowing and not the patient.'

'Danny's an unusual man, one of the finest men I've ever met and certainly the one of the strongest will. He's come a long way, from nothing, built up a fine business and now, at fifty five when he should be reaping the fruits he has this. And all he can think of is to spare his wife. It's a damn shame.'

'Yes,' said Milton and closed his notebook. 'I'm sorry about all that.'

'So am I.' Godfrey got up from his chair and waited for Milton to rise before he grinned. 'You must be a right awkward sod when you really get your teeth into something.'

'The trouble with this case is that there isn't anything to get your teeth into, as soon as you think you have, it all slips away.'

'I know the feeling. Give my regards to your wife, Arthur, and tell her from me that you're lucky to have her.'

'She knows that already.'

Milton settled himself down into his chair, at the side of the fireplace, neatly angled to give him a view of the television set. He eased off his shoes and loosened his tie; it had been a very long and tiring day, more than twelve continuous hours. His wife was in her chair on the other side of the fireplace, knitting and watching the Benny Hill Show at the same time.

'Enjoy your pie?'

'Great.' Milton got out his cigarettes.

'You smoke too much, Arthur.'

'I know, I walk about too much and all.'

'You don't feel ill, do you?'

'I'm all right.'

'You're not keeping anything back, are you?'

'Some hopes of that, you're the detective in this house. What are you on about?'

She held up her knitting and gazed critically at the stitches. 'It's just that I met Mrs Yelland and she mentioned that she had seen you in Dr Godfrey's waiting room.'

'I see.'

'Still, if it wasn't anything.'

Milton grinned and lit his cigarette. 'It wasn't but that

isn't going to stop you cranking on about it. I called on Godfrey for a few addresses.'

'I thought you got all those from the voters' register.'

'Doctors are more up to date,' Milton lied. 'He's a decent bloke, old Godfrey.'

'He's no older than you.'

'We had a smoke together, I suppose he can't when there's a patient around. What are you knitting?'

'A cot shawl.' She held it up.

'You were around there again today? How are things?'

'Mary's marvellous but Jim, he looks ill, dreadful, poor man. Judith is there now, she's going to stay with them until she has her baby. I think I feel sorry for her most of all, poor girl, it should be such a wonderful time for her instead of . . .'

'Yes, I should call round to see them, I suppose, but it's awkward, they'll have had enough of coppers.'

'You wouldn't be going as a policeman.'

'They'll still have had enough, maybe next week. Anyway, not tomorrow, it's the funeral.'

'I've ordered a wreath from us and I've said I'll go. I mean I would have gone up to the church anyway but Mary asked if I'd go with her and Judith because John, her husband, can't be there. He's had to go somewhere for his firm.'

'Where?'

'I don't know, somewhere where there's oil I think. He didn't want to go, he was worried about Judith, that's why he's brought her over to be with her mother. He's a nice boy, he's been very helpful.'

'He looked all there at the wedding; how old is he?'

'I don't know, not very old, twenty four or five, but he's very mature for his age.'

'He sounds like it.'

His wife concentrated on a particularly tricky part of her knitting and Milton reached to the back of his chair and slipped the official photograph of Monica Henekey from the inner pocket of his jacket. He held it on his knee so that he could study it unobtrusively. He knew a lot about this girl with the heart-shaped face, vivacious smile and ribbon across her hair. The date of her birth and the day of her death. What schools she had gone to, what sports she played, where she went for her holidays. And others knew a lot more; by this time Shenton would know every article of clothing that she possessed, the books she read, her friends and precisely where every one of those friends had spent that Tuesday night. He would know everything that there was to know, her taste in clothes, in food, in entertainment, her ambitions, perhaps even her dreams.

'I know you can't tell me anything really important, Arthur, but do you think that he will be caught soon?'

'I'm not likely to know. All I do is make up lists and check addresses. I'm a very small cog in all this. It's Shenton who knows.'

'Well, they must find him soon. I've never seen so many policemen in my life, in every street, calling at every house. Mary says that they've never stopped asking questions about Monica's friends, relatives, even her school-teachers.'

'That's Shenton, all right. He was like that in the old days. He accumulates facts like a sponge. Names, faces, habits, every possible fact. He'll know the lot by now, everything there is to know.'

Everything, he thought, except who killed her and why.

CHAPTER
TWELVE

The morning of Monica Henekey's funeral was bitingly cold and the wind, cutting across the cross-roads at the old town centre, hit Milton in the left ear like a chilled scythe. Both windows of the old, unmarked CID Vauxhall were wound down so that he and Sheehan could watch the pavements and street corners. They were both aware that they had no method of spotting Monica Henekey's murderer even if he danced about in the road in front of them, but orders were to watch for any men making their way to the church. Killers who attended their victim's burial were very rare, and those who made themselves conspicuous still rarer, but it had happened.

Sheehan took the matchstick that he had been chewing out of his mouth and threw it into the street. 'This is a bloody waste of time, if you ask me. I still don't know what unusual behaviour means; he's not likely to go by waving her drawers at us, is he?'

Milton grunted and looked at his watch. 'All right, pull over to the church and drop me by the gates. You can take the car on to the side road and wait on the other side of the churchyard, by the lychgate.'

'You want me to look around?'

'Yes, but stay close to the car. If anyone's coming for a sly look then that side road's as good a place as any. Just watch for the likely age group and check them out, no heavy leaning, just make sure that you know who they are.'

Sheehan fired the engine and drove carelessly across the crossroads to where the Church of Christ the Redeemer stood at an angle to the new shopping precinct: its two hundred year old spire dwarfed by the glowering cement block of a new hypermarket. The little crowd standing on the pavement outside the church was mostly composed of women with children under school age. There were only three men, one very old pensioner, the staff photographer of the local paper and a long, thin youth wearing a college scarf and duffel coat who was carrying the shopping bag of a much older woman: mother and son? Landlady and pliable lodger?

Sheehan pulled the car into the kerb and Milton got out onto the pavement: he looked at his watch, 11.27.

The crowd began to thicken, women came out of the shopping precinct and clustered in knots outside the church gates. A young, uniformed constable arrived and began to sort out the thickest group of people who were obscuring the run-up before the door of the church itself. He glanced sharply at Milton before giving him a small nod of recognition. A reaction came from the crowd as the leading car came over the crossroads—a towering Rolls Royce hearse with its roof banked with flowers—and then came the mourners in three big Daimlers.

Milton moved deliberately to the fringe of the crowd, turning his back on the church. There were a lot of people in the streets now, shopkeepers had come out onto the opposite pavement and Milton looked at them all very carefully but none stuck out from any of the others, none were markedly solitary. He turned back towards the church in time to see the coffin being borne through the church doors on the shoulders of the undertaker's assistants. The tall, hunched figure of Jim Henekey rose above the heads of the crowd, thick grey hair falling untidily over a bent head: a glimpse of Mary Henekey, swathed in black and then the slow plump figure of the other daughter, Judith. Then other less determinate figures, amongst whom he could not detect his wife.

He flicked his eyes back across the street and froze: an old 2.4 Jaguar had pulled tightly into the kerb immediately behind the cortège: the engine still turning over and the nearside passenger window fully wound down. Milton moved speedily across the pavement and put his hand on the door handle as he stooped to look directly into a round, moon face, with a much receded hairline.

'Who the hell are you?'

'Police, let's have your licence.'

'Bloody hell, all I want is . . .'

Milton snapped his fingers. 'The licence!'

There was a fumbling and then a torn plastic folder appeared—Arthur Freshman of 83, North Road, was licensed to drive Motor Vehicles in Groups A to K inclusive.

'Why have you stopped?'

'Because they're burying that poor kid. I'm paying my respects and if you're a copper why don't you do something useful like find the bastard who killed her instead of pouncing on me?'

'You're on a yellow line.'

'I'm not parked, I pulled in for a moment.'

'You're blocking the road so move it,' said Milton shortly, 'and right now or I'll move you.'

'Bastard!' The voice was piercing and Milton turned to face a sharp nosed woman wearing a headscarf. 'All right for messing motorists and decent people about but no bloody good with crooks or buggers who rape girls and kill them. No bloody good then.'

'Go away.'

'Useless bloody snotnose.'

'Just go away.'

The constable had moved closer and regarded both of them with a complete lack of expression. The woman turned her back and Milton looked round to see that the Jaguar had driven away. He took out his notebook and noted both the car index number and Freshman's name and address. The crowd outside the church was breaking up, moving slowly back into the shopping precinct: the few who looked at him did so with hostility.

Milton waited until the pavement had cleared and then went up to the church and round the corner into the churchyard: he stood for a moment at the West Door. Nothing had penetrated the old walls during the address but now the choir was singing, voices of youthful purity, the choir of Monica's school, piercingly beautiful in *Morning Has Broken*, the children's hymn.

He moved away from the West Door and walked along the path that led through the centre of the old churchyard, with the barely decipherable monuments to the Nathaniels and Emmelines and Jacobs and Ezekials who had died in faith and with the absolute certainty of bodily resurrection and life everlasting.

Sheehan was leaning against the bonnet, smoking a cigarette, which he dropped on the ground when he saw the look on Milton's face, they got in the car and Sheehan drove off without speaking until they had filtered back into the main road.

'Anywhere in particular, Skip?'

'Get the other side of the town centre.'

'There wasn't anyone,' Sheehan swung the wheel and went into a racing turn. 'Not a light.'

'Left when you reach the traffic lights and left again past the pub.'

'Up here? You paying a call?'

'That's right, past the lamp post, the one with the green door.'

Sheehan toed the car into the kerb. 'You want me to come in?'

'No, I'll not be long and if they radio us we're on our way. Oh, and give them this name.' Milton tore the page out of his notebook. 'Ask them to run a check. He was dodging about behind the hearse and in a Jag, he's somewhere in his late fifties.'

'He don't live here, does he?'

'Just radio it in and stay put.'

He went up the little garden path and banged his head on the hanging basket that dropped on a chain from the roof of the porch. He held his thumb on the bellpush for a long time before there were cautious movements behind the door. He faced the spyhole and spoke at the little square box beneath it.

'Hello Mildred.'

'Who?' came the muffled voice.

Milton took off his hat. 'It's been a long time but you remember me, don't you?'

The door opened. 'Of course I do, Mr Milton, is something wrong?'

'Not for you, Mildred; are you on your own?'

'Oh yes, come on in.' She held the door back. 'Go straight through, Mr Milton, I was just having a cup of tea.'

He went up the short hall and into an overcrowded living room. There was far too much furniture of an old-fashioned style: engulfing armchairs with arms almost a foot wide, festooned with cretonne covers and cushions: footstools covered with sheepskin, nests of coffee tables and a turkey carpet barely visible under thick rugs.

He slipped off his overcoat but it was still too warm, there were three radiators and a gas fire going full blast and none of the windows was open. A wing armchair with about fifteen cushions on it was set close to the gas fire and immediately in front of it an ornate colour television set flickered a children's cartoon.

Mildred swished by him in her cyclamen housecoat to a far door which opened into a tiny kitchenette. She left the door open and there were sounds of water and the clatter of cups. Milton fingered his collar in the airlessness.

'Take your jacket off,' Mildred appeared at the kitchenette door. 'I like to see a man looking at home.'

Milton took off his jacket; apart from the lack of oxygen in the air there was something comforting about this room; like a childish accumulation of goodies.

'Now then,' Mildred picked her way through the obstacle course of footstools and side-tables. 'You look tired, Mr Milton, are you still working those terrible hours?'

'Are you, Mildred?'

'You mustn't tease me, I'm retired now.' She settled back into her mountain of cushions and gazed fondly at him. 'It will be ready soon. I like tea to stand properly, don't you? It's been a long time since you've come to see me, Mr Milton.'

'Well, you've not been doing any harm, have you, Mildred? There's no reason for me to bother you.'

'You know what I mean, I used to like those little chats of ours, I like talking to intelligent men.'

'You say the right things, Mildred, your customers must find you very comforting; very good for their egos.'

'I wasn't giving you a sales talk, dear, well maybe a little but I really did enjoy our talks. I'm not in business any more, just one or two old friends. I've known them for years, and they're both gentlemen. I couldn't cope with the young ones now and they wouldn't fancy me, would they? I should think that they get it all for nothing these days, the poor things.'

'If you really have retired, you're doing all right on your savings.'

She hoisted herself up and traipsed back to the kitchenette again to return with a silver tray laden with a teapot and bone china teacups. 'I always liked pretty things as a girl, I never saw the point in having things that weren't pretty if you could have things that were.'

She set the tray down on one of the little tables. 'You haven't really called on business, have you, Mr Milton?'

'In a way, but my business not yours. You've read about Monica Henekey, the girl who was killed?'

'Dreadful, the poor child is being buried this morning isn't she? It must be absolutely terrible for her parents.'

'The man who did it is kinky, all he did was to kill her and take her knickers. We think it was someone that the girl knew, at least by sight, someone that she saw no harm in taking a lift from. He must have a reasonable looking car so it follows that he has a fair amount of money and he'll appear respectable, probably a family man. The papers are calling him a monster but I think that the people who know him, even if they have noticed something odd would never connect him with anything like this. I think he's probably looked upon as a quiet ineffectual sort of man; he probably picked the girl up by chance and then something gave way, he lost control of himself and panicked. You must know the sort of man I mean.'

'Oh dear!' The housecoat gaped as she reached down to pour out the tea and showed a plump white breast.

'We're checking at every house so everyone is going to be seen anyway. All I want is a hint so that when we do see someone like that, as part of the routine, we can check them a little more closely, ask one or two extra questions.'

'I couldn't talk about my friends, dear, not by name. I never have, you know, not since my sister passed on, dear old Jessie. We used to laugh about it occasionally but not really at them, you know, just about the funny things they got up to. I couldn't tell you their names, you do see that, don't you?' The deep blue eyes were moist.

'I don't think the man we want would be one of your

regulars, Mildred, that wouldn't be his style, but it's very likely you'll have heard about him.'

'I wouldn't know anybody like that. They call him the Beast and he must be, he's killed—I don't know how many. I wouldn't know anybody like that, Mr Milton.'

'Forget the papers, Mildred, the man who killed Monica is different, he's not a ripper. All I want is a hint, a middle-aged man who's kinky for young girls and don't tell me that they all are.'

'Well, they're not, are they, whatever pictures they put in the papers. It's funny you know, really, but mature men, real men, like women their own age, like their wives, but saucier. Rather what they would like their wives to be if they were more daring. They like to feel at home. Real men aren't relaxed with girls young enough to be their daughters, that's my experience. They like a change but not a ridiculous one, they like a nice place, they like to be comfortable and to talk about themselves. I've always thought a nice place was very important.'

'Well, you've got a nice place all right. You know, Mildred, you were born out of your time, you really belong to the naughty nineties. You'd have been the toast of the town then.'

'I'd have loved it then, all those beautiful styles and those lovely balls to wear them to, I had the figure for them too but I can't complain about my life, I've known some lovely people. I think you would have suited those times too, you've the figure for evening dress.'

'Don't disarm me, Mildred, what about this man I'm looking for?'

'I really don't know anybody like that, dear, and I really have retired: ten, even five years ago I had a very select clientele, no one with really peculiar ideas.'

Milton sighed. 'Other policemen aren't like me, Mildred, they're not so patient and they've got bigger feet. They wouldn't tread anywhere near as gently over this carpet of yours. Old Maurice is still running the Haystack and you still go up there for lunch: you may be running at half-speed but you still know what goes on.'

'You wouldn't send another policeman around to see me really, would you dear? It's not nice to threaten me.'

'You flirt beautifully and I enjoy it just as I always did. We're not going to fall out, are we?'

She poured herself another cup of tea. 'You're a naughty man, I never could resist a really masterful man. There is a creature called Anthony Wright who holds parties where girls dress up as all sorts of things. A really dreadful man, I saw him once, very tall but thin with long, stretchy arms like rubber bands: I'm told he shows dirty pictures but I don't really know. I've never had anything to do with him.'

'Where does he live?'

'I really don't know, dear, I only heard about him in passing.'

'Anyone else?'

'Of course not, this is a respectable town. It's terrible really, such a waste, no real friendship in it, is there, no dignity.'

Milton laughed and got up. 'You're a great woman.' He checked his watch against the gilt clock, the dial of which was supported by two figurines. 'That's a very fine clock.'

'I've had it almost two years, that shows how long it is since you've come to see me. Isn't it lovely?'

'A present from a friend, but you wouldn't tell me.'

'It doesn't matter now, that's one of my little rules, it doesn't matter once someone's passed on. That was a present from a very dear friend of many years, a real man of great taste, a real gentleman. Mr Craddock.'

'You mean Alderman Craddock?' An immediate mental picture of the late Alderman Craddock shot into Milton's mental cinema, the long ascetic face, cold eyes, bristling eyebrows and sharp chin and always the hard white collar, funereal suit and gold watch chain: hospital governor, member of the watch committee, donor of a public drinking fountain. He laughed until he got the hiccups and then had to find his handkerchief to wipe his eyes. 'God, I can't imagine it, he always looked as if he'd creak with rust if he ever bent.'

'He was a fine man, a real gentleman and a man to the end. He was with me, you know, on the Saturday, the day before he passed away and he died beautifully, in his sleep, no fuss or bother to anyone. He died like a gentleman.'

'He must have died happy and all.'

When he got back to the car Sheehan was on the pavement stamping his feet down in order to keep the circula-
tion going. 'Jesus, Skip, I'm dying of frostbite; is that old
girl Mata Hari, or something?'

'She's a whore,' said Milton, 'a good clean, honest
whore.'

'At her age?'

'Don't get uptight; at any age.'

'Where does she put it about, the Darby and Joan clubs?'

'In her own little way,' Milton settled himself into the
passenger seat, 'she spreads a bit of happiness and sorts
more problems than ten crime squads put together.'

CHAPTER
THIRTEEN

Shenton was irritable when he arrived at the station on the Monday morning. He had driven to his home for only the second night since Monica Henekey's death, but he had slept badly. He put his heavy document case with the wad of reports that he had read the previous evening, onto his desk and considered sending down for someone to bring him some coffee, but then changed his mind. He sat down at the desk and then got up again. He lit his pipe but it drew badly, because he had rammed the tobacco in too tightly. He eased it upwards in the bowl with the end of a matchstick and seared the tip of his thumb. It all increased his irritation and he looked coldly at Graham as he put his head round the door.

'Yes?'

'I can come back.'

'What is it?'

Graham came into the room. 'There was an incident last night, in Greenacre Park, over by the railway station. A girl was going through it around ten o'clock, and a man came out of the bushes at her.'

'He attacked her?'

'She got away, she was already running when she saw him, she's a nervous sort of girl. She got off a train just before ten, her boyfriend saw her onto the train but he lives in town and she lives on the other side of the park. Going through it saves her a twenty-minute walk but she was nervous so she ran through it, and when she was about half way through she heard a noise, a snapping she says, like a twig breaking. She looked round and saw a shape coming out of the bushes, so she ran like hell. She can't describe what she saw, she ran all the way home, collapsed and her mother rang us. Six cars went to the park and combed every inch of it but they found nothing.'

'So?'

'We've had trouble in Greenacre Park going back two years. It could be the girl's imagination but I believe her. I think it's the same man who did the others, and that dragnet or not he's still on the prowl. He can't resist it.'

'And he's the man who killed Monica Henekey?'

'I wouldn't know about that but I'm bloody certain he's the creep who's done six other girls in that park and he needs nailing. I want that park sewn right up until we have him. If he's on heat then I don't reckon it will take long, maybe tonight.'

'Perhaps.' Shenton took great care in retamping the tobacco down into his pipe and struck a match. 'I agree that there should be a watch on that park, but the squad is pretty stretched.'

'I'd sooner use my own men. I've already had a word with Christine Wren—she's willing. I reckon a car at each end and another couple on the side roads.'

'Who will you put in charge?'

'Myself.'

'I see.' Shenton sat down at his desk and nodded towards the other chair. 'You could control this far better from your desk but I suppose you're as fed up with sitting at a desk and looking at paper as I am. What sort of watch do you want?'

'I thought start around nine o'clock and then send her through at twenty minute intervals. I think the bastard gets in and out of that park over the side railings. There are a lot of dark patches along both sides so I want a good watch along both of them. I thought cars in the side roads, facing the park, each with night glasses. As I say, I want to be among them unless you think something more important is likely to come up.'

'No, and as you say, you can always be contacted by radio. I'll be here tonight myself.' Shenton moved the document case round on the desk and opened it. 'I spent most of last night going through these questionnaires. I was at it until past midnight and there's nothing in any of them. Plenty of discrepancies, dozens of justifiable callbacks, but no real meat, nothing to make you feel as if you're on to anything.'

'It's bloody frustrating,' agreed Graham. 'All we've turned up is the usual parlour intrigues behind the lace curtains, like that thing Dewsbury. Nothing that gives you the old feeling, that makes your nose twitch. I'd give a lot to have just one good, solid lead, something to really get hold of, and really wring the blood out of it. All this frigging about, with old women of both sexes and what they thought they might have heard or didn't quite see, is driving me straight up the wall.'

'I didn't sleep too well,' Shenton continued. 'I can usually switch off but not on this one. It's the girl, the sort of girl that she was and the way that she got into that car; it doesn't jell with the North London killer at all. I can't put my finger on it, but the pattern is wrong, the whole feel of it is wrong.'

'But, like you said, whether it is him or not, he still killed a sixteen year old girl.'

'But if it wasn't him then he could be anywhere, miles away, and he won't be sitting still, he's due for another one, any time now.'

'But you've got the rest of your squad on that and six decoy teams out. No one could do any more, you can only do your best, you can't wet nurse five million people.'

'Yes, I'm taking it personally and that's always a mistake. Let's get on to something worthwhile.'

'The uncle. Edward Henekey is clear, he was with a woman who puts it about from a flat over by the industrial estate. She's got a couple of kids who were taken into care this week by the council. She's been on the game for six months and Edward Henekey is a regular customer. The squad turned her over and checked the neighbours, Henekey was with her all right, no possible doubt about it. He's a nasty little bastard but he's not our bastard.'

'How many more alibis have we got like that?'

'There's a lot of it about. The list Milton got from the doctors has still to be checked out but he's put in a special note. I'll see him if you like.'

'No, let's hear what he has to say.'

Graham picked up the telephone and passed the order down to the CID room. Milton appeared two minutes later to stand stiffly in front of the desk.

'Sit down,' said Shenton. 'Did you have any trouble with the medical men?'

'They were all very co-operative.' Milton passed over his lists. 'Fifty three men in all requested medical attention or asked for medical certificates for those two days. I did not record those who had things like broken legs. I've checked the list with Sergeant Charles and there were twelve who had the opportunity to be on the North Road at the relevant time. I have marked them with the questionnaire numbers and attached details from their statements. Three of the twelve have previous convictions but only one, Green, has convictions for a sexual offence.'

'Who is Green?'

It was Graham who answered. 'A great lump who lives with his parents over a fish and chip shop in the High Street. He's mentally defective; his convictions are for interfering with children, ten or more years ago. He's already been seen, I saw him myself, he was on the local offenders list. His mother swears he was in all night.'

'Did you believe her?'

Graham shrugged. 'Green looks what he is, a drooling idiot. I don't see the girl getting into a car with him.'

'What about these other two?'

'Thompson and Gains, sir.'

'OK.' Shenton lay back in his chair and put his pipe at an angle. 'Let's hear about them.'

Milton cleared his throat. 'Graham Thompson, age thirty-five, salesman. Drives a Ford Escort, colour grey. Lives Wellclose Crescent, garden adjoins that of the Henekey's. On the night of the 18th he arrived home at 5 p.m. and left again at 7.30 p.m., according to him he went to call on two customers—he sells domestic freezers—but neither of them were in. At least they didn't open the door to him. He arrived home at around 10.30. There's no corroboration, his wife was in bed when he came back. The wife is pregnant: there is one child of eighteen months. He called on his doctor on the morning of the 19th, complaining of a sore throat and stomach upset. He did go out later that day, on his rounds again. He is physically capable, six feet in height. He has a local reputation as a womaniser. His convictions are theft, and the driving away of a motor vehicle without consent as a juvenile, and as an adult he has two convictions for driving without due care.'

Shenton looked at Graham and raised an eyebrow. 'I don't know him,' said Graham, 'but he sounds as if he's worth a look.'

Milton turned the page of his notebook. 'The second one is Wilfred Gains, age fifty-one, he's a welding foreman and drives a Ford Granada, metallic bronze. He has four daughters, two of them married and two at home, sixteen and fourteen. The sixteen year old was one of Monica's classmates. They live in Mott Street which is three turnings from the Henekey home. Gains went to his doctor on the 19th and complained of stomach pains. His doctor says that it happens every two or three months, because Gains has an incipient ulcer. He has put him on a diet and told him to lay off the beer but with little effect. Gains says that he worked late on the 18th and went on to have a drink afterwards, he went to three pubs but he's unable to state the times he was in them, so there's no corroboration. He got home around 11.00 p.m. and he says that he drove along the North Road on his way home but that he saw nothing. He's more than physically capable, 6 feet 4 inches and weighs around sixteen stone. His previous convictions are for careless driving, assault on a man he had an argument with in a pub and one for being drunk in a public place.'

'Would the girl have known him?'

'She was friendly with his daughter but it's quite possible that he wouldn't have recognised her or she him in the street. According to the statement he made at his house interview, he said that he thought he had seen Monica but it was more than a year ago and she was in school uniform.'

'Anything else on this list?'

'I have a note on one other name, Daniel LeRoy, I have him listed because he meets all the relevant criteria but his physician, Dr Martin Godfrey informed me, in confidence, that LeRoy has cancer of the stomach and that the medical attention in his case was for painkilling injections. LeRoy is very concerned that his wife should not learn of his condition until it is absolutely necessary.'

'When you say he meets the criteria, what does that mean?'

'He drives a silver grey Jaguar 4.2 and he was out in it that night. He attended a meeting of the British Legion Welfare Committee of which he is a member and afterwards drove a disabled member of the committee home to Grant Road on the other side of the High Street. He returned to the British Legion Hall because he had left a document case there but after picking it up he left almost immediately. All that is corroborated. After leaving the hall for the second time he drove home up the North Road, he lives in Goff's Walk, which is the other side of the common and the golf course. He says he got home around half past ten and that is not corroborated because his wife did not arrive home until after midnight. She was at a committee meeting of her own; she's the chairwoman of the local children's fund. In his statement LeRoy said that he drove along the North Road on his way home and that he would have passed the tennis club but says he noticed nothing. He's a big man, 6 feet 1 inch tall and the observer noticed nothing wrong with him, he has him marked as well-built.'

'He sounds a remarkable man, knowing what he has and attending welfare committee meetings and giving other people lifts.'

'Dr Godfrey used the same word, remarkable. LeRoy is fifty-five and a sales director. He is acquainted with the Henekey family; he has served on the same British Legion committees as Jim Henekey and they have visited each other's houses. In the normal way that does mean he warrants a back check but in view of Dr Godfrey's remarks . . .'

'Yes,' said Shenton, he put both his elbows on the desk and let the bowl of his pipe hang down so that the smoke drifted up over his shoulders. 'It does have to be checked, I think you should see his wife, Milton; emphasise that it is purely routine. Just put it to her that her husband was out that night and so we have to check on him, see how she reacts.'

'Yes sir.'

'The other two, Thompson and Gains, can go to the squad, together with the rest of your list. Have you anything to add on any of them?'

'Well, it's hardly a lead but I have marked number 8 on

the list; Jackson, Anthony Jackson, he's a draughtsman around forty. Married with one son of fourteen. He lives next door to the Henekeys and the wives are friendly but not the husbands. He went to his doctor on the 19th complaining of stomach pains and sickness. Dr Ranjam diagnosed gastric enteritis and Jackson has not worked since. I marked him because Ranjam volunteered the remark that Jackson was a morose man. I asked him what he meant by that and he said "a man without friends". On his questionnaire, Jackson says he left home on the 18th around seven o'clock to go to see a football match, but he went on his own so there is no corroboration. He returned home around 11.00 p.m. and went straight to bed because he felt ill. He says that he travelled by the North Road and saw nothing. He is 5 feet 5 inches but very thickset. The observer describes his attitude as wary.'

'Interesting.' Shenton got up from his desk and walked round it to look out of the window. 'What sort of car has he got?'

'A Volvo, dark green.'

Shenton nodded several times and then turned round to look at Graham. 'A good hard look, then, at Mr Jackson. That was a good job, thank you Milton.'

'Thank you, sir.'

'Report back to Mr Durant,' Graham told him. 'But hold yourself available. I want you for a special watch tonight.'

'Yes sir.'

After Milton had left, Shenton picked up the list and rifled through the pages. 'He really did do a good job.'

'He's all right, so long as he's pointed in the right direction. A plodder; never knows when to change gear.'

CHAPTER
FOURTEEN

Detective Policewoman Christine Wren was an attractive woman. In her neat dress, raincoat and fashion boots, she could have been a receptionist, courier, sales executive or superior secretary. Dress like a career girl she had been told and that was easy because she was one.

So here she was and all very boring it had been so far; walking through the centre of the park at half-hourly intervals. For the fifth time she entered the park from the direction of the railway station, conscious of the night glasses that were watching her progress through the first plantation of trees. The first time that she had walked through the park, two youths had appeared from one of the side paths and had whistled and danced about in front of her, trying to make her change direction but neither of them had touched her. On the fourth trip a small, wizened old man had appeared, suddenly and startlingly, from a clump of rhododendrons. He had shouted something completely incoherent and waved his fists in the air as he followed her through to the end of the park. A patrol car had picked him up in the street and he had turned out to be a decrepit alcoholic with a long history of mental illness who, despite the stringency of the dragnet, had managed to get into the shrubbery to sleep off a drunk.

And so, for the fifth time, she approached the centre of the park and, despite her knowledge of the men circling the park to protect her, the knot in her stomach still tightened. However attentive the watchers, they could not be really close if the trap was to work and if anything was going to happen then it would happen fast, frighteningly fast. During the seconds that it would take for the watchers to reach her anything could happen, literally anything.

She was past the centre of the park now and entering the last curve of the path before the final stretch and the lamps standing outside the gates. She relaxed and slackened her pace; when she reached the gates she crossed the road to the bus depot, walked through the bus garage and only then doubled back through the staff entrance to the waiting Q car. The watch was being kept by Sheehan and Milton; she joined Milton in the rear seat.

'I guess that's it,' said Christine taking up the coffee flask.

'Notice anything?' said Milton.

'Not a damn thing. For the last fifty yards there were only the squirrels.'

'He's there.'

Christine choked on the mouthful of coffee that she had just taken; a peculiar sensation spreading up from her stomach.

'Take it easy,' said Milton, and offered her a cigarette. 'We couldn't see him either. Purple three called up from the other side of the park. A man was seen jumping the boundary fence along the back road. He spent a lot of time walking up and down, waiting for the traffic to clear so that he could do it on the sly. They saw him go in and they watched him through the first lot of shrubbery but then they lost him. A man about six foot wearing a long dark coat.'

'I didn't see a thing, had no idea; you know, feelings about anyone being there.'

'We didn't see him either and we had the night glasses on—didn't even see a leaf flutter. I doubt he saw you. He went in about the time you started, so if he made for the path he'd have reached it after you passed. But he's there, we've got a full watch all the way round now and he hasn't come out.'

Christine swallowed hard. 'What now?'

'I've been on to Mr Graham, he's coming himself and all available cars are being sent in, but it's up to you.'

'I've said I'll do it.'

'Take your time,' said Milton, 'it's different now we know he's there for sure. Like so far it's been a sort of a game but now it's for real. There's nothing against you saying no. We can always go in and get him as he is, that could be enough.'

'No,' said Christine, 'it isn't and you know it isn't enough just to find him in the park.'

'You think about it. You don't have to make up your mind until the brass gets here.'

Graham came in a convoy of four cars that disposed themselves at the other end of the service road. He already had a full scale map of the lay-out of the park. 'Purple three reckon he went in here, level with the trees, it's a straight line to the road in the middle, it's marked.'

'It's called the midnight path,' Milton told him.

'The papers will love that. If it's the path he was making for, the shortest route would bring him out past the pond, about here.'

'That's where the shrubbery is the thickest,' said Christine, 'where the girl ran from him the other night.'

'If it's him,' said Graham, 'that's where he'll be.' He looked at Christine. 'It's up to you.'

'I've already said . . .'

'Let's be fair about it, you're scared. So would I be and so would anyone else who's got all their marbles. We'll have cars both ends and they'll be there in seconds, but seconds can be a bloody long time. I can't get anyone in the park until you start walking, if I do we'll lose him. We won't be able to reach you before he gets his hands on you and that's not bloody funny. I'd as soon go for the bastard now and take my chances on what I squeeze out of him, so you think about it.'

Christine thought about it. 'I'll go.'

'You've got a lot of guts,' Graham told her. 'Now, keep your personal radio on transmit, don't try to talk but keep the channel open. If you see him, shout, scream, anything, if you can; otherwise just drop it, we'll hear that. If he reaches you don't concentrate on anything but saving yourself.' He looked at her reflectively, 'He goes for the neck, keep one hand up there, if you can.'

'Yes sir.'

'We'll come in fast, like a bat out of hell.'

'Yes sir.'

'All right, Christine, when you're ready Milton will take you back. Good luck.'

They took her back to the edge of the park and waited for the radio link to tell them that everyone was in position.

Milton looked at her as they sat in the car; she showed no

obvious sign of strain, her face was placid but there was a tightness about her. Milton tried for a few words to tell her something comforting, a few words of reassurance but although he searched his mind he could find nothing to say.

Sheehan behind the wheel seemed uneasy, he shifted his huge shoulders and he turned once or twice to look at them but in the end he said nothing either.

The handset of the car buzzed and Milton leaned forward to pick up the receiver. 'Graham,' came the voice, 'go now.'

'Right,' said Milton and got out of the car; Christine followed him and took a deep breath. To Milton's surprise, Sheehan also got out of the car and stood beside Christine Wren, dwarfing her by his enormous bulk. 'Here,' he said, producing his truncheon, 'hold it like this and as soon as he touches you, a back hander with the end, like that, straight in his goolies.'

Christine took the truncheon awkwardly and tried to smile. She waited until they had reseated themselves in the car before she walked to the entrance of the park.

She forced herself to slow her pace but even so it was a fast walk; the heels of her white boots clicked provocatively on the asphalt of the path.

As soon as she passed through the gates of the park the light level dropped remarkably. The trees and high bushes that were placed at either side of the path immediately inside the gates filtered out the light from the street lamps along the pavement outside. There were lights set to illuminate the path that led through the centre of the park but they were widely spaced at intervals of a hundred yards or more. A terrible unease started to creep along the line of her spine. The muscles of her stomach contracted and despite herself the footsteps became more rapid and louder. The light that did come in from the road threw fantastic shadows across the path from the trees, shadows that seemed to move, to dance.

She was approaching the centre of the park now and the lamp that stood at the side of the path; immediately beyond it the path swept round a thicket of rhododendrons which threw the path beyond into deep shadow. This was the point, the centre, the logical place for any attacker to lie in ambush. She tightened her grip on Sheehan's truncheon and tried to remember what it was that he had said, she fumbled for the personal radio and kept her thumb well down on the transmit switch. She was under the lamp, feeling even more vulnerable, and then past and away from the full glare of the lamp and towards the shadows; she was level with the thicket and then past, out of the deepest shadow. She had an urge to laugh, she had been so certain that the attack would come in the darkest part of the park. Perhaps there would be nothing after all, and she would walk to the end of the path, what an anti-climax!

She never heard him coming, not even with every nerve tightened, every sense screwed up to maximum awareness. There was no rustle as he left the bushes, just a frozen moment of something being frighteningly wrong and then a terrible arm came across her throat from behind—as hard and as brutal as a band of steel. The surprise, as much as the force of it, took Christine off her balance and she dropped her radio. She tried to stab backwards with the truncheon and she felt it strike home but it made no difference; the pressure about her throat remained as brutal as ever. She was vaguely aware of foliage pushing against her face and she tried desperately to reach up to get the man's fingers but all her fingers scrabbled against was some kind of slippery plastic. There was a pounding in her head and she could feel herself blacking out: she made a final gigantic effort and stabbed backwards with the heel of her boot and this time she did hit something.

Then she was on the ground with earth and leaves pushing against her face. The arm was no longer around her throat and she opened her mouth but she could not cry out, she could not even swallow. There was a sudden rush of cold night air across the tops of her legs and something like claws were digging into her thighs forcing open her legs. An unbearable weight bore down into the centre of her back and then, suddenly, a light was shining onto her, a terrible, piercing light, much too powerful for her to look into. There was a confusion of noises but the loudest of them was the pounding of her own heart.

As Christine moved away from the car, Milton radioed to Graham that she was on her way and Graham came back with an immediate acknowledgment and a repeat of his instructions that all task force sets were to put to receive and that no transmissions were to be made on Channel 7, in any circumstances, until further notice.

Sheehan had wound down his window and they could hear Christine's heels clicking on the asphalt but they faded once she had passed beyond the screen of poplar trees that guarded the gates of the park. Milton held the receiver near to his ear so that he could continue to hear the footsteps. Sheehan was tense, his hand hovered over the gear stick and his huge shoulders hunched themselves over the wheel. Milton concentrated on the footsteps, they were firm and rapid, she was right not to dawdle, it would be too suspicious: they sounded right, the sort of pace a girl would walk at going through a park at night.

'She'll be about half way,' said Sheehan.

Milton did not answer, he thought he could detect a hesitancy in the footsteps, but no, they were going on. Then suddenly they stopped dead, there was absolutely nothing and then there was a scraping noise, a sort of scuffling, as if leaves were being rubbed together. Was it possible that she was kicking her way through a pile of old leaves? He moved the volume control up to full pitch. His tension must have communicated itself to Sheehan because he touched the accelerator more heavily and brought up the note of the engine.

'Christ,' said Milton. The crash as Christine Wren's personal radio hit the asphalt almost split his eardrum.

'Move,' shouted Graham over the car radio and Sheehan let up the clutch with such savagery that the car seemed to leap from the ground. As the car shot through the park gates he put up the full set of headlights and it took no more than three seconds for them to reach the central lamp: as they swung broadside at the slight bend Milton had to shield his eyes from the impact of the headlight from Graham's car coming from the opposite direction. Sheehan swung the car back on course again in a half racing turn to avoid the other car and nearly sent Milton through the windscreen as he braked. Sheehan was out of the car at the same instant as he switched off the engine.

When Milton got out of the car the first thing he saw in

the beam of his torch was Christine Wren lying on the edge of the path, her head and shoulders were hidden in the undergrowth: her legs were sprawled apart and her skirt was wrenched up above her thighs with the remnants of her tights clinging pathetically to her knees. Graham was slightly ahead of him and moved back the broken ends of the bushes to reveal her head. They both turned her over and Milton brushed the earth and leaves from her face: as the light shone into her eyes she tried to raise an arm to shield herself.

'It's all right,' said Milton, 'it's all right.'

'Stay with her,' said Graham and was gone.

There was a lot of noise coming from further in the undergrowth, lights were flashing and many branches and twigs were being snapped.

Milton pulled down her skirt and helped Christine to a sitting position. 'Are you OK to stand?' he asked her and she tried to answer but all that came out was a croak, but she did try to get up so he helped her to her feet and then held her whilst she vomited at the edge of the path. Milton gave her his handkerchief and led her down to his car: she looked very pale. He got her into the back of the car and picked up the handset of the car radio. 'I'm getting an ambulance.'

'No,' it came out as a croak and she had to put her hand to her throat.

'Don't be silly,' he put through the station call sign and was making his request when the bushes broke open again and the others came out onto the path. Graham emerged backwards and after him came Sheehan who had his jacket half off and his hair all over the place, he had someone by the arm and neck, the second crewman from Graham's car had the man's other arm but it was only a token effort: Sheehan's grip looked as if it could only be broken by a cold chisel. The other two from Graham's car followed with their platform torches; one of them carrying some kind of black hood.

Milton tried to see the man but all he got was a glimpse of a tight white face and a round bald head, as bare as a billiard ball, as the man was hauled past to the rear of the other car. Graham came over.

'How are you?' he asked Christine.

'I'm—I'll be—' the voice was a husky whisper.

'I've called up the ambulance,' Milton told him.

'Here.' Graham produced a pocket flask and poured a shot into the removable base. 'Don't tell me a thing, a bruised throat is bloody painful.'

Christine obediently drank the brandy and handed the cup back to Graham as the ambulance swung alongside Graham's car.

'I don't want to hear a peep from you until midday tomorrow. There's no hurry, not now we've got the bastard.' Graham helped Christine towards the ambulance and then beckoned one of the crewmen from his car. 'You go with her, Perry.' He walked Christine to the doors of the ambulance and saw her inside. 'I never meant him to get that close,' he said to her when she was seated, 'but I had to be sure. You're a very brave girl.'

The doors of the ambulance were closed and then it moved off with its blue light flashing. 'She did well,' said Milton.

Graham nodded briefly and went across to his own car and leaned through the open rear door. 'Has he got anything on him?' he asked Sheehan.

Sheehan jerked the man upright. 'All he's got on is this plastic mac, he's stark bollock naked underneath.'

'No pockets? Nothing round his neck?'

'Yeah.' Sheehan gave a savage jerk which brought the man's head forward so that it struck the back of the driving seat. The plastic raincoat gaped from the neck and from the back tab hung a tape with a single key. To Milton, looking over Graham's shoulder, the man's pallid body emerging from the black raincoat, had the look of a monstrous, shelled slug.

Graham took the key. 'You take Castle in your car, Milton, and then pull the others off watch. Hamilton can resume his normal patrol but the rest of you I want up Perry Lane: have a good look at all the houses in the lane and in the turnings that come off it, there's only three of them. I want a note of all houses with a light showing, that's all, no calls, just a note of the addresses. When you've got that you bring it back to the station and leave it at the desk. Sign everybody off, they can all go home, including you.'

'Yes, sir.' Milton got into the driving seat and waited for Graham's car to move off before he engaged gear.

'A right, lovely bastard all round,' said Castle, 'with his spike and that hood.'

'Did he give much trouble?'

'He tried to use the spike so Sheehan thumped him. By Christ he thumped him, took the sod right off his feet. Old Sheehan took it real personal.'

'He fancies Christine Wren.'

'That straight? I never heard . . .'

'Leave it,' said Milton and swung the wheel as they reached the corner of the park.'

The man sat in the interview room, slumped in his black plastic raincoat, like some kind of obscene sausage. Sheehan stayed very close to him, perched on the edge of the table, his right fist bunched ominously on his knee.

'We'll have that coat off,' said Graham, 'get a blanket, Sheehan.'

'Right.' Sheehan got off the table and went out.

Graham took one of the wooden chairs and turned it round, put it down in front of the man and then settled himself astride it with his arms folded across the back. He stared straight into the colourless eyes and they held his gaze for a few seconds but then they moved away, first to one side and then to the other.

Sheehan came back with a cell blanket and the man allowed himself to be manoeuvred so that the plastic raincoat was stripped from him. He did not resist but he made no effort to help. Sheehan threw the blanket across the shoulders and only then did the man move of his own volition, holding the edge of the blanket to wrap it around his body.

'Are you a nudist,' Graham asked, 'or did you reckon on the exercise keeping you warm?'

The eyes flickered but there was no answer. Sheehan took the raincoat and deposited it in a forensic bag. Graham nodded and Sheehan sat down at the table with his notebook.

'OK,' said Graham, 'it's 23.47 hours on the 8th October. Present is Detective Superintendent Graham, which is me, Detective Constable Sheehan, and you. We'll put your name in later and if you think that playing dummy is going to stop us from knowing what it is, you haven't got a prayer. Until we get it you can't even ask for legal representation and you're going to need plenty of that.' The eyes were as expressionless as inkwells. 'You are under arrest for the assault and attempted rape of Policewoman Christine Wren and the attempted murder of Constable Sheehan. You are not obliged to say anything but anything you do say will be written down and given in evidence.'

Graham took the key from his pocket and dangled it over the back of the chair. 'Whether you talk or not doesn't matter a tinker's cuss because this key is going to lead us straight to your bolt hole. You got into the park over the railings in Perry Lane, so we'll start with the houses that back onto the lane and if we get no luck there then we'll check the houses beyond them. It won't take us long. I wonder who'll open the door to us.'

The man put his face down into his hands, propping his elbows up on his knees. Graham promptly knocked the elbows away.

'I haven't brought you in here just to look at the top of your lousy head. Sit up!' Sheehan got up from the table and heaved the man upright by his shoulders.

'Listen carefully,' said Graham. 'When we find the house we're going to tear it apart, any little souvenirs you thought it was safe to keep, we're going to find. We'll find something and the other girls you've done will identify you when we put you up. I'm going to nail you on them all. You can have it dumb or you can have it crying. I don't give a brass shit how you have it but I'm going to have *you*.'

The man opened his mouth but nothing emerged. He got to his feet, the blanket falling away from his body. Sheehan was also on his feet and had him in an armlock.

Graham remained in his chair, looking up at the six foot column of flesh that swayed in front of him. 'I'm going to have you,' he said in the same voice, 'speak or bloody not, I'll have you!'

The man came crashing down on the table. The blanket

fell away and his naked body fell heavily. Sheehan still had him by the arms.

'Come on,' Sheehan heaved him up.

'He's fainted.' Graham got up and scowled. 'Lay him out and get that blanket over him, and mind his head, I don't want any bruises. I'll get a police surgeon.' He wrenched open the door of the interview room and almost ran into the reception area. Newcombe got up from behind the desk.

'Get Dr Crombie.'

Newcombe started dialling the number. 'An ambulance as well, sir?'

'Yes.' Graham lifted the flap of the counter and went through. 'I'll speak to him myself; give Sheehan a hand.'

'Yes, sir.'

Newcombe hurried a little, when he entered the interview room he regarded the heap of humanity in Sheehan's arms with sardonic interest.

'Who hit him?'

'No one.' Sheehan had his arms under the man's shoulders. 'cop hold of his legs; it's like handling a lump of jelly.'

Newcombe obliged. 'Is he a hop head?'

'Christ knows, he flaked out when Graham said we'd have his bits and pieces.'

'He doesn't look like much, does he?'

'Like a heap of shit.'

'Sling him round here, by the door.'

'Mind his sodding head. We don't want to hand it to his brief on a bloody plate.'

'Tempting though, ain't it!'

CHAPTER
FIFTEEN

When Shenton entered the station's CID control office at eight thirty he found Graham sitting at his desk. The office was a shambles and as Graham struggled to his feet Shenton noted the bloodshot eyes, stubbled chin and sweat drenched collar.

'You're going to make yourself ill, pushing it like this.'

'I know but . . .' Graham made a vague gesture towards the litter of notes that he had been working on.

'I've done it myself, it's always tempting to make one last effort, to wrap it all up for good.'

'I just knew that there was something if I could only get to it. You're right, I couldn't let it go. I had to have something to really nail him. I couldn't let the bastard slip off the hook.' He looked down at his notes. 'I think I've got him now.'

'Would it help if I ran through them?'

'Yes, sure, I'd be grateful.' Graham bundled his notes together into a pile on the desk. 'I've got to—I won't be long.' He crossed to the door and went out, stumbling a little as he hit the edges of the door frame.

Shenton emptied the ashtray into the waste basket and then used one of the crumpled pieces of paper to clear the top of the desk of spilled ash before he sat down. Then he produced his spectacles, settled them on his nose and read Graham's notes. He read swiftly, racing his eye past the preliminaries, clinically noting the essential points.

Police surgeon Dr Crombie examined suspect at 1.03 a.m. Apparent faint during interrogation: possible malingering. At 1.20 a.m. suspect delivered to Draycott Hospital and held for observation. Suspect conscious, pupils dilated, clinical examination discounted concussion: no apparent connection with blow struck in self-defence by DC Sheehan.

5.30 a.m. Houses in vicinity of Perry Lane checked against list of those showing lights at 23.35. Two addrèsses in both categories. 6.00 a.m. second address 87, Greensward Avenue checked, key fitted front door lock: house entered, clothes and wig on hall stairs: no occupant in house: central heating plant in operation. Neighbours informed name of house occupant as Kevington; also agreed general description of Kevington which meets that of suspect with exception of baldness.

Graham came back with his hair combed and Shenton took off his spectacles and smiled.

'First class!'

Graham sat down in the other chair. 'It was easy once we knew where to look and once we got in it was all there, his clothes and the wig. No wonder the bastard got away with it for two years: the back of that house is only thirty yards from where he went in over the railings. So long as he could make it back home he was fireproof. Different clothes, a different man, especially with that wig. All I did was follow my nose.'

'Yes.' Shenton recalled the remark that Graham had used to dismiss Milton and he suppressed a grin: they had far more in common with each other than either would ever know. 'He said nothing at all?'

'Not a blind word, here or at the hospital. When he came round he just lay like a waxwork. Crombie said he was OK, had a good look at his eyes and said he wasn't—what's the word—catonic, he wasn't catonic.'

Shenton nodded. 'And the hospital is sure that the blow Sheehan struck had nothing to do with it?'

'They're not that definite; they're waiting for the neurologist's report but they reckon it's a form of induced hysteria. A kind of retreat, so that he can't be questioned, he was bent anyway and knowing he was lumbered could have sent him over the edge. It was the houseman I talked to, not official, just between him and me.'

'It sounds reasonable. Did he live alone? What did the neighbours think of him?'

'He never spoke to them and none of them had ever seen him without his wig. He's got a wife, the neighbours reckon she has a dog's life. There's also a married daughter up north somewhere. The wife wasn't in because she's got an old mother who lives in Torquay and she goes down there four or five times a year to sort the old lady out. The dates need sorting out but it's obvious that he only went on the prowl when she was away.'

'Does she know?'

'No, I'm seeing her tonight. All she's been told is that her husband had a blackout and has been taken to hospital. I'll meet her train, it gets in at ten.'

'There's got to be a reason for all this.'

'As much as there ever is. I got a bit of it from the family doctor, he knows Kevington: the only local who knew he was bald.'

'He was willing to make a statement?'

'No, but he reckoned the wife had had the hell of a time and he wanted to make things easier for her with us. I haven't got round to writing it up. I don't know if I can put it into a report anyway. The gist of it is that Kevington's fifty one and has been a mess since he lost his job around four years ago. Before that he worked for a big construction outfit, he's a qualified surveyor and he worked at the same job for twenty five years until he got the chop. I don't know why, it could have been an ordinary redundancy but whatever the reason it all starts from then. He was treated for hypertension, stomach pains, insomnia and melancholic depression. His doctor persuaded him to enter Ramsden as a voluntary patient. That was after he made a scene in the Social Security Office; his unemployment benefit had been cut down because of the time he had been drawing it and he had a go at a counter clerk because he said she was laughing at him. It was around then that his hair started to fall out, in handfuls.'

'What did the Ramsden people do?'

'They couldn't find anything really wrong but they did diagnose him as being a cyclothermic personality which, as far as I understand it, means someone who swings from normal into deep depression for no reason. The doctor said that it can be easily controlled by drugs but Kevington discharged himself from Ramsden and cut himself off from everybody. His wife came to see the doctor but Kevington refused to take any further treatment and the doctor said he couldn't do anything about it: Kevington wasn't certifiable.'

'That doctor must be feeling vulnerable.'

'He doesn't want to be quoted but he did say that he wouldn't have been surprised if Kevington had committed suicide. What shook him was that he had attacked anybody. He said that losing a job in middle age is always the hell of a blow and quite naturally results in some kind of depression in the same way as any other kind of emotional shock. It means that you've got to come to terms with what you really are and we all know how painful that is. In Kevington's case he must have been a bastard to start with, envious and mean minded, were the words that the doctor used, and instead of sorting himself out he ended up hating the world.'

Graham shook his head slowly as if trying to clear his brain. 'Anyway, it's all up to the headshrinkers now, whatever he's got, they'll find a long word for it.'

Shenton nodded and swung himself back in his chair. 'He certainly needs putting away but it has no connection with the Henekey case. I take it that there's no question . . .'

'No, he lost his car when he lost his job and he hasn't had one since. The one thing that the neighbours did all agree on was that he hasn't had any kind of car for the past four years. It was a company car and he had to hand it in when they unloaded him. That must have hurt as well.'

'He wouldn't add up anyway; we're looking for someone very different.'

'Not all that different.'

'A different kind of relationship. Monica knew the man who killed her, there's a connection between them.'

Graham started to say something but instead yawned, so violently that he very nearly dislocated his jaw. He lurched to his feet. 'I'll have to go home. I'm dead on my feet and I've got to see Kevington's wife tonight, right off the train before anyone else gets to her.'

'Of course,' Shenton watched him leave and then took up the wad of statements that had been deposited into the in-tray. He started to read the first one but then his attention wandered, his mind returned to what he had said to Graham. Was the man he wanted so different from

Kevington? There must have been something at the back of his mind, something his sub-conscious was trying to tell him. Kevington had hunted in one place, returning to it again and again, hidden and watchful as he waited for the weak to be isolated. He had hunted like a wolf and he had been trapped because he could not alter his hunting ground. But the other one, more dangerous by half, he was not like that, was he, he was like, what? Ah, yes, like a fox because he took his prey on their own terrain, and afterwards, like the fox, he concealed his own tracks with infinite cunning. You can trap a fox, he reflected, but only if you know where he is likely to strike. Otherwise he has to be chased all the way back to his own earth and that is only possible if you can pick up and then retain his scent.

His reverie was shattered by the telephone bell on the special line which by-passed the switchboard. It was a call from the Chief Inspector whom he had left in charge of the East London headquarters.

'Jordan, sir, I hope I'm not interrupting anything.'

'What's happened?'

'Nothing dramatic, sir, but I think it could be significant. The number three decoy team think they had a sighting last night. I've been assembling the details and the more I put it together the closer it seems to come, the description of the man . . .'

'What description?'

'They all agree he was 5 feet 9 inches or 5 feet 10 inches, dark hair neatly cut, and looked like an office worker. The Photofit they've come up with is almost an exact copy of the one by that student's landlady.'

'I'll come over.'

'They lost him,' said Jordan apologetically. 'None of them were within twenty feet of him but it's possible—he could be back. There's nothing definite but it's the way it comes together.'

'What time does the team come back on duty?'

'One o'clock.'

'I should be there around half past, have them ready for me.'

Shenton replaced the receiver and then used the second telephone to order his car. He asked for Graham but he had already left the station. He hesitated about leaving a message then he shrugged and told the switchboard he would return before evening. After all, it was more than a hundred to one that there would be anything in it.

When Milton entered the CID room to sign on for the afternoon shift he discovered an extremely irritated Inspector Durant attempting to regularise a fragmented duty rota and allocation of enquiries list.

'Miss Wren is all right,' Durant told him. 'The hospital sent her home this morning but she won't be in for the rest of the week. Sheehan did twenty hours so he's booked off for the rest of the day and Mr Graham won't be back until late tonight. I know he wants you to do callbacks but I can't find the priority list. Did he give you any notes?'

'Only for LeRoy, sir, but that's not special, just one to work in when I'm over that way.'

'I'll check with the squad, he might have passed it to them, anyway they'll have the right names. Stay on call, Charles has been screaming for help, you can give him a hand for an hour or so.'

'Yes, sir.'

Sergeant Charles gave him a sardonic greeting when he entered the incident room. 'I heard you'd taken up park keeping.' His cadets grinned happily. 'I bet it pays better.'

'What doesn't?'

'Bugger all.'

'What's on,' asked Milton, 'the same old rubbish?'

'It's mail call time. Since Shenton's press appeal we've been getting a hundred-odd letters a day and they've all got to be read and docketed. The likely ones go to Shenton. So, pay attention, you lot, any letter that makes sense you put in the check tray and stick a docket on it saying in about ten words what it's about. The obvious nut cases go into the crank file. If you don't know the difference then you check with either me or Mr Milton. We're experts on nut cases.'

Charles produced a heap of letters, all opened with their envelopes pinned to them. He passed them out in handfuls.

'Unbelievable,' he said, shaking his head. 'It happens every time but it's still bloody unbelievable. Where the hell do these people come from?' He picked up the top letter from his own collection. 'This pronk reckons he can tell us the car so long as we line up all the cars in town and then he'll walk along them and point out the right one with a hazel twig. So long, that is, as we give him one of Monica's shoes to hold while he's doing it.'

'Why can't he do it standing at East Street crossroad?'

'The vibrations are all bloody wrong.'

'This comedian saw it all in a dream. The girl was lured to an old dark house by a little bald man whose name begins with A. And afterwards he took her body up to the common on a hand cart.'

'Here's a right one! This bird wants us to give her the minute of the hour of the day that Monica was born. Then she'll work out where her destiny collided on the day she died and then all we've got to do is to find the birthday of the bloke we want and she'll work out the conjunction. The stars never lie.'

'Jesus.'

'Who's got the bloody crank file?' Charles shouted.

'This might be one.' The cadet next to Milton passed over the letter. Mrs Pelling had written to explain that she was separated from her husband but that she had to see him at irregular intervals because they jointly shared the custody of their son who was in the care of Mrs Pelling. At around half past nine her husband, John Pelling, had visited her unexpectedly. He had been drinking and he had wanted to see his son who was asleep in bed. His wife refused and her husband had become abusive: the argument had culminated in his giving her a black eye. John Pelling had left the house shortly before ten in a highly excited state when his wife had threatened to call the police.

He was, his wife pointed out, a violent man of bizarre sexual habits. He drove a car which was changed frequently as part of his employment as a company representative. When he left she saw him drive off in the direction of the North Road.

'You reckon?' Charles asked.

Milton nodded. 'It's a hundred to one that the poor bitch just wants him leant on but it needs checking all right. And put him on the CRO list: if he's that free with his fists it's likely he's got a bit of form.' He picked up the first of his own letters and this offered the aid of the cards. At a seminar in Bridlington and at the exact moment of Monica's death which the writer of the letter said was at 10.46 p.m. the black ace had paired with the red queen. At the same instant a wineglass had split across its stem and shattered when no human hand was near, a sure indication this, of dark forces. Seek, said the letter, seek the man who had played the role of knave in Monica Henekey's life; for the card that had been turned as the wineglass shattered was the knave of spades, so that the red queen had lain between the black ace and the knave.

'What are we supposed to be looking for?' came from one of the police cadets.

'The jack of bloody spades.'

'How much?'

'Nothing,' said Milton and picked up another letter.

CHAPTER
SIXTEEN

Shenton sucked at the mouthpiece of his pipe and then put it down in the large glass ashtray. The sour taste of nicotine remained in his mouth and he picked up his cup of coffee, grimacing when he found that it was cold.

'Of course, it could be a waste of time,' said Chief Inspector Jordan.

'True,' Shenton brought a small tin of mints out of his pocket and began to suck one rather noisily.

'It was the number three team, Llewellyn, Selby and Miss Cullen. They've been working the underground stations for six weeks but last night was their first at Gant's Hill.'

'Yes?'

'The trouble was that he wasn't interested in our girl. If they'd been able to concentrate the whole team on him from the beginning we'd know the lot by now.' Jordan moved uneasily under Shenton's steady gaze. 'But he was definitely there for something and when Selby saw him follow this other girl . . .'

Shenton gave himself another mint. 'When did he know that?'

'At the traffic lights, Miss Cullen turned off at the arcade and the suspect went over the crossing, close behind this other girl.'

'I see,' Shenton was thoughtful.

'I've got the team hanging on in the briefing room.'

'Let's have them in.'

As Jordan rang through on the intercom, Shenton took up his pipe from the ashtray and thoroughly banged it against his fist to loosen the dottle. As he restuffed the bowl with tobacco the members of the decoy team filed into the room. Sergeant Llewellyn was a hulking figure, Selby short and rather slim; Policewoman Marilyn Cullen was a pert blue-eyed blonde.

Shenton nodded to each of them as they came up to the desk. 'Sit yourselves down,' he said pleasantly. 'Mr Jordan has told me what you got up to last night. It's possible that it could be the break that we've all been waiting for: what we have to decide now is just how likely that possibility is.' He found his matches and started to build up a small smoke screen. 'You can smoke if you want to. Now, Miss Cullen, did you see this man at all?'

'Yes sir, I saw him as I came up from the line. It was the third time I had done that since we started the patrol at five o'clock and I am certain that he was not there on either of the previous trips. He was standing at the back of the ticket machines. That was the only time I saw him but I was able to see him quite clearly.'

'Thank you. Sergeant Llewellyn?'

'The man was in the booking hall for about ten minutes in all, sir. I particularly noticed him because he fitted the general description of the suspect in the other cases. When I first saw him he was on the far side of the booking hall, by the wall, at the side of the entrance. It is possible that he came up from the line in the middle of a bunch of passengers but it is my impression that he came in from the street. I saw him move from the wall and come over to the ticket machines. He stood there while three separate trainloads arrived and he watched all the passengers. When Miss Cullen came up he moved in front of the ticket machines and fell in behind the people walking out of the station. It seemed to be going all right until Miss Cullen turned off into the arcade. I had a feeling about him and I told Selby to stick.'

'You did well. How close did you get to him Selby?'

'I got within a yard of him, sir, when we crossed over the main road at the traffic lights but he had his back to me and once we were across I had to drop back. It was on the other side that I could see that he was following this girl, a blonde wearing a purple coat. He watched her all the time but at no time did he try to approach her. He got ahead of her on two of the roads that they crossed and then dropped back behind her again. He was quite close to the girl most of the time but he was very cunning about it, a lot of the time he kept to the other side of the road. I stayed about thirty

yards behind him. When the girl went into the house he was
on the opposite side of the road and he had to wait for some
cars to pass before he was able to get over, but by that time
the girl was inside. He went up to the front door, there are
two steps up to it and a sort of porch. He looked as though
he was going in and I thought I would have to do something
about it but then he came out onto the pavement again. He
stood outside for a minute or so and then he moved off up
the road. He didn't come back my way, he took a sidestreet
and circled back towards the main road. I started to close
up on him again because there were more people about but
he jumped onto a bus that was standing at the traffic lights.
The lights changed just about the same time as he got onto
it and the bus pulled away. I saw him sitting down by one of
the windows, it was on route a hundred and twelve but I
could not see the number.'

'Do you think he could have seen you?'

'No sir, while he was after the girl he was concentrating
on her too much to notice anything else and afterwards I
kept well behind him. When he jumped on that bus he had
no way of knowing that the lights were going to change that
quickly and as he sat down he didn't look round or towards
me at all.'

'What did he look like?'

'Five ten, medium build, dark hair cut quite short, clean
shaven and very neat appearance. He was wearing a dark
suit, collar and tie, black shoes. He was well dressed and
well groomed, a typical rising young executive type. He
certainly fits the general description and the Photofit made
up by the landlady of that Ledger girl is a close match for
him.'

'Miss Cullen?'

'I agree, sir, he was immaculate.'

'Sergeant?'

'I only saw him in profile, but I did have him under
observation for more than ten minutes and in my opinion
he is either the man that landlady saw or his twin brother.'

'Thank you.' Shenton turned to Jordan. 'What do we
know about the girl?'

Jordan opened his notebook. 'Sylvia Jenkins, twenty-
two, teleprinter operator for an insurance company in the

City. Her family lives in Herefordshire and she goes back there at weekends; during the week she stays in her bed-sitter. She's between boy friends and she doesn't go out much.'

'You've seen her?'

'No, she'd already gone to work. I got this from the landlady. I've got the name of the firm she works for but I haven't contacted them. I have got a Q car in the street in case she comes home early but I haven't done anything else. The other decoys are still out but apart from a few oddballs there hasn't been a thing, not up to this strength.'

'What time does she get home?'

'She comes off the train around six o'clock.'

Shenton looked at his watch. 'That doesn't give us much time.'

'No sir, we could grab him if he tried to get into the house. Or, we could have someone walk with the girl from the station but then he wouldn't try anything and it's likely he'd be off for good. All we could do then is to pick him up in the street and try to shake something out of him. We'd at least know who he was.'

'We need time,' said Shenton, 'twenty four hours at least. Keep that Q car where it is. Selby, I want you to go back to that station, not in the station itself but outside and if he turns up then watch him. Report back if you can but take no chances of him seeing you, keep as far back as possible; lose him rather than have him see you.'

Selby rose. 'Yes, sir.'

'And you Sergeant, get up to this insurance company, take Miss Cullen with you and bring the girl back here. We'll ring through to let them know you're coming. Give the girl the outline, show her that picture but keep it as vague as possible. Try not to frighten her but don't let her out of your sight and get her back here just as soon as you can. Don't let her talk about it to any of her workmates or telephone her family.'

When they had gone Jordan got to his feet. 'Shall I ring the company sir?'

'Yes, get the head of her department and make sure that the girl's there. Keep it light, spin any tale you like but make certain she stays until Llewellyn gets there.'

Shenton watched Jordan pick up the direct line telephone and commence dialling and then, on an impulse, he brought up his document case from the floor and removed the file that he had been carrying about with him for so many months. It contained duplicate copies of the key crime reports and statements that he had read and re-read a thousand times. His eye skimmed the pathetic list of names, Gloria Harrow, twenty-four, machine operator, raped and strangled. No witnesses.

Geraldine Cooper, twenty-six, pharmacist, raped and strangled. No witnesses.

Heather McWilliam, twenty-one, secretary, Australian national, raped and strangled. No witnesses.

He turned the pages swiftly, opening the file fully at the crime report on the fourth girl; Caroline Obvert, nineteen, drama student, raped and strangled. Body completely unclothed, and found by other occupants of house within fifteen minutes of death.

Witnesses: other occupants of house. First witness saw girl enter house at approximately 6.40 p.m. also saw man enter house immediately after girl. Second witness saw man going down stairs from Obvert's room at approximately 7.05 p.m. Third and fourth witnesses entered house as suspect was leaving, he pushed between them in order to reach the street.

All four witnesses were struck by the incongruity of the man in this particular house. They agree he was 5 feet 9 inches or 5 feet 10 inches, middle or late twenties: wearing a dark business suit, white shirt, dark tie. Hair dark and cut to a conservative length. His appearance was in marked contrast to all other habitués of the house who were predominantly student and bohemian. No CRO photograph picked by any witness.

Shenton riffled further into the file. Irene Ledger, twenty-three, physiotherapist, raped and strangled. Body found immediately after death.

Witness: Mrs Georgina Cummings, fifty-nine, landlady of Irene Ledger. At approximately 6.45 p.m. was in the hallway of her house when she saw a man coming down the stairs from the first floor. On being challenged the man said that he was a friend of Irene and had seen her home. Mrs

Cummings was suspicious, she took a strong motherly interest in the girl and had met all her friends. She asked the man his name but he pushed past her and left by the front door. Mrs Cummings immediately went up to the girl's room and found her body.

Mrs Cummings describes the man as being approximately 5 feet 11 inches, medium build, aged approximately twenty-eight. Eyes brown, hair dark brown brushed flat across the forehead and cut level to the ears: excellent teeth, full lips. He was dressed in a dark blue suit of good quality and cut, pale blue shirt and string tie: black shoes.

She stated that he smiles readily and could be considered charming, his voice is cultured and without any noticeable accent. Was unable to select any CRO album photograph; assisted in compilation of Photofit which also agreed to by witnesses re Obvert.

Shenton laid aside the file and picked up the Photofit picture.

'Was that OK, sir?'

'What?'

'To have the supervisor keep the girl in her own office.'

'I'm sorry, yes, of course. Is she upset?'

'I don't think so.' Jordan nodded towards the Photofit. 'Funny the way he keeps to the same pattern.'

'How close is that Q car to the house?'

'I don't know, ten, twenty yards.'

'Pull it back, out of the street. No, wait, get one of them into the house, discreetly, so that he can see the hall.'

'And Selby, shall I—?'

'How good is Selby?'

'First class,' said Jordan definitely. 'He's missed promotion on his paperwork but on the job there's no one to touch him, he's the best thieftaker I've got.'

'Then keep him where he is. But get that car out now.'

The bungalow was the same as any other in the cul-de-sac. When Milton rang the bell, the door was opened immediately by a man who looked as if he had been closely shaved within the previous thirty seconds. His chin shone, the dark hair was brushed tightly to the head, flattened by a great amount of oil. The black eyes gleamed like damsons.

'Police.' Milton showed his warrant card. 'May I have a word with you sir.'

'It's ridiculous, stupid.'

'We have a report that we have to check. It would be a lot better to do it inside.'

'It is absolutely stupid.'

'It's quite simple,' said Milton. 'Part of the general survey that we are doing, we have to check everything. Our information is that you were not at home during the evening of Tuesday the 19th, between the hours of nine until eleven p.m.'

'It's malicious.'

'There's nothing malicious about it. All I want is a straight answer to a straight question. The information we've been given is either right or wrong: were you out of your home on Tuesday the 19th between those times?'

'I did not mean that you were being malicious. I meant that the person who gave you that information is malicious, he knows very well where I was.'

'And where was that?'

'Passing the word.'

'What word?'

'The word of Lord Jehovah.'

Milton looked into the gleaming black eyes and had a sinking feeling in the pit of his stomach. 'You were making religious calls?'

'What other calls could I have made?'

Milton did not tell him. 'Do you have a list of the houses you called at?'

'I can tell you the roads. I only note the addresses at which I receive an encouraging response.'

'Did you have any of those that Tuesday night?'

The lip curled. 'No.'

'Was anyone with you?'

'I carry out my witness alone. The great Jehovah . . .'

'I suppose,' said Milton, 'that you were allocated these roads from your headquarters—from Kingdom Hall.'

'Yes.'

'And you went there, I mean the area, by car. You would have driven from here to the other side of the railway station and then parked and made your calls on foot.'

'That is quite right. I did drive in my own car, I parked it to the rear of the railway station and returned to it after I had made my calls. I drove back to Kingdom Hall, I arrived there at approximately ten thirty. I returned home at eleven.'

'You would have driven along the North Road both times. Did you see on that road or anywhere else that night anything that you would have regarded as being suspicious? A girl and a man in a car? A girl who possibly looked distressed . . .'

'There are always girls in cars with men.'

'Did you know Monica Henekey?'

'No, but I have seen the posters.'

'So you would have noticed her?'

'I had not seen the posters then. I would not have looked closely at a car that passed me on the North Road. I may have seen her in a car while I was on the North Road. It is very possible but I would have had no reason to scrutinise a car that was passing me. I cannot remember any cars that may have passed.'

'Can you remember anything unusual?'

'Nothing.'

'You did not stop for any girl, or notice a girl standing at the bus stop outside the tennis club?'

'I saw no one.'

'Was anyone at home when you arrived back at eleven o'clock?'

'I live alone.'

'Ah.' Milton turned the sheet of his notebook. 'Is that so? According to the Town Hall's voting list you are married and live here with your wife.'

'My wife is not here. I live alone.' The eyes opened wider. 'I live alone, sergeant, my wife had insufficient faith, and she has removed herself. She will either return when she has truly rejected the false snares of this world, or— . . .'

'Or?'

'Or she will remain in the abyss.'

CHAPTER
SEVENTEEN

'She agreed?' asked Chief Inspector Jordan.

'She did.' Shenton sent up a great cloud of smoke from the end of his pipe and peered placidly at the collection of files and cards that were scattered across the long conference table. 'After she got over the shock, she agreed. A very nice girl, quiet but determined.'

'Selby is still at the station, the man hasn't showed.'

'He won't now, bring Selby back. Let us have the map, he's cunning and now that he knows the house he doesn't need to pick the girl up at the station. He won't go into the house unless he knows that the girl is there. He's got to be pretty close behind her to know the room, but he doesn't have to follow her all the way from the station.'

'He's not been sighted near the house.'

'He wouldn't wait outside, but further back, somewhere inconspicuous, a bus stop, or shop doorway. He's cunning, this one, very cunning and very careful.'

'He could have called it off if he was there tonight.'

'He could but he's a plotter and he'll calculate that the girl's gone out on a date or that she's sick. I think he'll be back tomorrow. But it has to be tomorrow, if she doesn't appear then it's more than likely that he'll run.'

'You approve of Miss Cullen for the switch?'

'She'll do very well, a wig and the same coat; from the back that's all he needs to see. The point is that those are the things that he's using to pick her out in the crowd, he'll be concentrating on them.'

'The girl could put him off, if she's nervous.'

'I emphasised to her that it was important not to look round or do anything unusual. She saw that straight away.'

'And blanket cover all the way?'

'It will have to be, right from the station. It's not likely that he'll pick her up there but we've got to cover it, and it will be the rush hour.'

'That should make it easier, we can get lost in the crowd.'

'No man to move up more than one street, a hand-over point at each corner. That means nine hand-offs and there isn't much time to work that out.'

'I'll get Llewellyn onto it. I thought I'd use three women in the team, Sergeant Clough does a very good young mum bit with a pram, leaning in to tuck up the shawl while she uses a radio.'

Shenton nodded. 'And how will we set out the mobiles?'

'After the girl's left the station, the back-up car is to come out into the main road from the arcade. It's the mini that's tricked up to look like a television repair van and I'll be in the back. It should pass the girl twice but otherwise it will be on the parallel roads. Then three unmarked mobiles, one following me up but well back, one parked beyond the house and the third in the next street ready to pull in from the other end.'

Shenton swung round in his chair. 'I'll be there, in my own car but well clear, somewhere in the High Street. What about the house itself?'

'It's tricky, he's got to be pretty close behind her if he's going to follow her to her room. He must have seen her start to go up the stairs last night, so he knows she's above the ground floor, maybe he knows she's on the top floor. I don't think so but it's possible. As I see it, we've got to lead him to the girl's own room and that's up both flights of stairs. There are three doors coming off the hall, two on the left and the one on the right which goes into a sort of cubby hole and then down into the basement where the landlady lives. We could have our girl in there, for her to step out as the other one steps in. The trouble is that he'll have to pass it.'

'You think he'll notice something?'

Jordan shrugged. 'It depends how close he is: there's plain glass in that door: he must have been peering through it the other night. And the door isn't latched at that time because so many people are coming and going. We'll need a bit of time for Cullen to get into the girl's coat.'

'True. Let him see the girl go in and have Miss Cullen come out with a parcel, let him see her walking away from that door with a parcel and have a notice stuck on the door, listing rules about keys or bathtimes. Something to suggest that it's an office. He'll creep by it carefully enough then.'

'Good point.'

'How wide is the staircase?'

'It's pretty narrow and so are the landings, just two doors on each. The girl's in a room of her own, the smallest, the other room on that landing isn't much better but I'll have three men in it. There are six girls in the rooms on the ground and first floors. I'll have them cleared out.'

'I don't like that. We don't know anything about this man. He could be a local, he's careful and he might have ways of checking. However discreet, he could see something.'

'There's nowhere else to hide the squad.'

'A man in the room, and a good man. So long as we can find somewhere to put him, he'll have the element of surprise. Which way does the girl's room face?'

'To the rear, it's above the area steps that lead down to the basement steps, about forty feet or so, but you'd have to lean right out of the window to see them. We'd have him if he jumped.'

'And the roof?'

'No chance, it's tiled, high pitched and there's no way to it from that room. His only way out is by the stairs or the window.

'So, once he's gone up from the hall there's no way he can see the street: we could bring the cars up.'

'We could have men in the landlady's room, in the basement and bring them up once he's bitten. If he goes up those stairs we've got him. Guaranteed.'

'It sounds all right.' Shenton stroked the side of his nose with the bowl of his pipe. 'Only one way in and only one way out, down two flights of stairs.'

'It's not worried him before. He's confident of knocking them off without any noise and he relies on speed, does them and then down the stairs and away. That's probably part of it, knowing how close other people are, even the risk of being seen, it's probably part of the thrill.'

'I think you're right.' Shenton sat back in his chair and drew gently on his pipe. 'What we have to hope for now is that wherever he was tonight he didn't get turned off the idea or see some other girl that takes his fancy.'

'So long as it is him.' Jordan put his large hands on the table and looked at them reflectively. 'Like you said there could be a dozen reasons why a man should follow a girl.'

'I know I said that but the more I think about it the more certain I am that this is the one. I've got a feeling about him, like your friend Selby. It all fits in with what we know about him, young, quick and very, very sly. He has a lot of cunning, animal cunning, like a fox. There's a smell to him.'

'Once he gets to the room it could be tricky. Once we lift him we've got to break him or get something from his house. Do we lift him as soon as he gets to the room or . . .?'

'Or does he have a go at Miss Cullen?'

'He kills bloody quickly from what we know, straight for the throat.'

'It's a risk, there's no way round that, if the girl opens the door to him. If she doesn't and we lift him on the stairs, it could be dodgy, all we'd have is trespass. But a blow to the throat, I don't like that. If she turned away from him, offered herself, he'd have to grab her from behind and so long as our man is quick—but he's got to be really quick.'

'Llewellyn can take anybody.'

'It's speed that matters. And what about Miss Cullen? It takes the hell of a nerve to turn your back on someone like that.'

'She's got plenty of guts.'

'Then it's her decision, we give it her without trimmings and if she's willing then OK. If not then we take our chances on breaking him.'

'Right sir, shall I put it to her?'

'We both will.'

'And the man for the room?'

'I'll think about it.'

The evening light was brilliant but by the time Milton reached Goff's Common a cold wind was blowing in from the golf course and Milton was glad of the warmth of his overcoat. The hedge running along the side of the road was broken in many places and it was no longer possible to fix with any certainty the exact point at which Monica's body had lain.

He looked across the common to the range of the golf course but no players were in sight, the only figure on the skyline was that of a lone dog sniffing at the lip of a bunker, lean and forlorn.

Broad Walk adjoined the golf course, a discreetly private road in which the houses all lay well back and were difficult to see beyond expansive lawns and thickets of trees. This was the territory of privilege, of condescension and cut-glass decanters and cocktail parties attended by Lords Lieutenant and Chief Constables. Unknown territory for a beaten-up detective sergeant.

The LeRoy house had as its nameplate a piece of shingle that hung on little chains inside a drive of smooth asphalt inset with white stone chippings. The house was Georgian, not particularly large but well set, framed by the velvet greenness of the golf course that flowed beyond it, and with space and freedom at either side of the house. No lean-to or bicycle shed here. It was self-confident affluence, all the way from the natural, hand-made bricks, to the wrought iron carriage lamp that served as a porch light.

When he rang the bell the door was opened by Mrs LeRoy herself who was slightly taken aback when he produced his warrant card. She was, possibly, fifty, but a well groomed, active and very personable fifty. Her grey woollen dress fitted closely and her figure was that of a girl of twenty five.

'How can I help you?'

'It's routine,' Milton told her. 'A routine check, every statement that we take has to be checked as much as possible.'

'Of course, I can see, that must be most important. Please come in.' She led the way into a room that ran the whole length of the house and ended in double French windows which opened out onto a patio. A long mahogany table was at the far end and there was an open writing case with several neat files. 'I'm afraid that Daniel isn't here. He's in town as a matter of fact, and I don't really know . . .'

'It was you I hoped to see, Mrs LeRoy.'

'Then won't you sit down, please do, but how can I possibly help?'

'Your husband has said that when he arrived home that night there was no one else here.'

'That is so. I was attending a meeting of the Branton Education Committee, I am one of the school governors. After the meeting I gave another member of the committee, Mrs Cousins, a lift to her home and once there we discussed a number of other matters. I spent some time with her, drinking coffee and so on. I got back rather late.'

'Your husband said after midnight.'

'Yes, that would be right. I can't swear to the exact time but it was after midnight, certainly. I'm afraid I can be of no help to you at all, Mrs Cousins lives over in Radlett and I drove nowhere near to the North Road or the common.'

Milton considered how to phrase the next question and decided to do it straight. 'Could you describe your husband's demeanour when you got home?'

'Oh dear,' Mrs LeRoy gave a little laugh. 'I see,' she gave him a tentative smile and then grew serious. 'The honest answer is that he was in rather a state. I had better explain that my husband has not been well for some time. His visit to London today is for a medical reason, to see a specialist, because of sudden attacks of pain. They come quite without warning and they are very worrying. At such times he is naturally not himself, in fact he is very distressed. He had such an attack that night. When I arrived he was in here, sitting at this table, looking rather ghastly: he was over the attack more or less but completely drained and I helped him up to bed. We should have some staff here, of course, to look after things, but good staff is so difficult to come by and au pairs are useless. So, the truth is that my husband was distressed when I returned home that night but with very good reason.' She flashed him a brilliant smile.

'That is a very honest answer,' Milton told her. 'Mr LeRoy did not mention being unwell in his statement.'

'Danny absolutely detests being ill, he has always been impatient with any kind of illness. This ulcer of his has only reached this stage because he ignored the symptoms for so long. I do hope that he has learned sense now.'

'Did you know Monica?'

'I've seen her many times. She was an absolutely delight-
ful girl, quite the most charming young girl that I have ever
known. I only knew her parents slightly, Jim Henekey
came here sometimes and Mary once worked for my husband, you know.'

'No, I did not know.'

'It was only for a little while, years ago when they were
going through a bad patch. Jim—Mr Henekey—came here
because he and my husband knew each other through the
British Legion. Not close friends but they have known each
other a long time, back in the days when my husband had
his own business. He brought it up from nothing, he
worked very hard and made a great success. Then he
amalgamated and that has meant, well, all this.' Again that
thousand watt smile. 'Jim Henekey did not do so well. He's
willing and I'm sure he does his best but that isn't always
enough, is it?'

'No.'

'In fact, I may as well tell you my husband went out of his
way to help Jim. He felt sorry for him. Danny would never
tell you this himself but if it wasn't for him the Henekey's
wouldn't be anywhere at all today. A lot of people think
that my husband is a hard man, Mr Milton, you know, the
self-made tycoon, and all that, it creates a lot of jealousy.
They have no idea of what he is really like.'

'No,' said Milton, 'I'm sure. A woman in your position
must know a lot of people, Mrs LeRoy, you must have your
finger on the pulse of general feeling. I was wondering if
you had any ideas about what happened. Any idea, however vague.'

'Well, no, it was a maniac, surely, the man who's killed
these other girls.'

'What I really meant was do you think that Monica would
have gone with a man that she did not know?'

Mrs LeRoy got up and stood looking out at her immaculate garden for several minutes. 'I hadn't thought, I mean
. . .'

'Yes?'

She turned back and looked at him with troubled eyes.
'Monica was a very nice girl, a serious girl but reserved, and
very shy with strangers. I was going to say that she would

never have gone with a stranger but that must mean that it was someone she knew.'

'Yes,' said Milton, 'that's exactly what it means and I agree with you, Monica would never have willingly got into a car with someone that she did not know. But have you any idea at all who it could have been?'

'No.'

'A guess, however wild.'

'No, I can't think of anyone. You knew her too, Mr Milton, can you think of anyone?'

Milton sighed. 'No, I can't, and that's the trouble.'

The man that Shenton finally selected to stake out Sylvia Jenkins's room was Detective Inspector John Purchase from his own crime squad.

Purchase was only half an inch above the regulation minimum height and of slim build but it was a very wiry build and, at the age of thirty two, he was in superb physical condition. He still played wing three-quarter in the divisional rugby team and he held a black belt in Judo but, more importantly, he had five commendations; three for the single-handed arrest of violent criminals and two for the excellence of his detective work. John Purchase was a bright boy who was going places.

'I have no reason to believe that this man is likely to be armed,' Shenton told him, 'but it is something that we have to consider.'

'I don't want a gun, sir.'

'No, but you might need something, he could carry a knife. He's always used his hands so far but he could well carry something, in case he runs into trouble, they often do.'

'As I see it, sir, the thing is to hold him as soon as he makes a move on Miss Cullen. I should have the element of surprise and if I get a good grip there shouldn't be any trouble about holding him. I won't need to hang on for long.'

'No, that is certainly true, once he goes into that room, we move in. We'll be very close.'

'I'd prefer to wear my track suit. I'll be able to move quicker and it's less likely to catch on anything.'

'Miss Cullen is a very brave girl.'

'I know sir, and I know this man is quick. I know he's got to get his hands on her but she is going to be ready for him, none of the others were. I'll take handcuffs, if it comes to it they'll do to clout him with: they make a very good brass knuckle.'

'I'm sure,' said Shenton.

Milton was surprised to see Mary Henekey in the front garden of her house. She was wearing a black skirt and sweater but she had tied a yellow silk scarf around her head and she was doing something with the rose bushes that shielded the front of her house. She looked up as he came level with her and she blinked as the sunlight struck her full in the face and even in that harsh light she was a strikingly handsome woman. How old would she be, forty two, three?

'You're making me feel guilty,' he said. 'My wife's always on at me to do something about our roses, but I must do it too soon or too late. They never turn out anything like yours.'

She smiled. 'It's a knack.'

She met his eye frankly but there was something that puzzled him: the smile held at the corners of her mouth but there was wariness.

'Has anything happened, anything new?'

'I'm afraid not.'

He was very close to her now: her eyes had changed, she relaxed as if with relief. He must be imagining it. She moved slightly, looking past him to wave to a woman on the other side of the road.

'I meant to call round before to see you and Jim but . . .'

'You don't have to say anything, Arthur, I know what you want to say but there aren't any real words.'

'How is Jim?'

'Better now, he's still on pills to help him to sleep but he's almost his old self now. He's gone back to work.'

'And how about you, Mary, really?'

'Ah,' she turned away to pull at loose tendrils from one of the rose bushes. 'I live from day to day and then there's Judith, you know, my eldest, she's having a baby.'

'Yes,' said Milton, 'Margaret was telling me.'

'She's much too young, but they're not kids at nineteen any more, are they? They're mature women, in my day we were still kids but as I was saying, I'm glad that she's having this baby, it's—I don't know how to say it.'

'I know what you mean.'

They stood for a time in silence and when Milton tried to catch her eye she was looking off into the distance: her face caught by the cold sunlight. It gave her face a golden overtone so that she looked as though she had been cast in bronze. When she did finally meet his eyes it was as if she had returned from a long journey.

'It will pass,' he said.

'What?'

'Nothing lasts, the good or the bad.'

'I know.'

'We will find him, you know, however long it takes.'

Her eyes went blank. 'Does it matter? It won't make any difference now.' She made a visible effort to control herself. 'Don't take any notice of me. It's just that I want to forget. I know you've got to go on, you and your Mr Shenton and all the others, but it won't bring my Monica back, will it? Whatever you do, nothing will ever ever change that.'

'No,' said Milton, 'nothing will ever change that.'

He tipped his hat and walked on up the road with its sparse laburnum trees, bathed in the autumnal sunlight. He admired Mary Henekey as he admired anyone with dignity, particularly when they retained it in adversity, but there was a nagging, niggling thought that she was somehow too controlled. He tried to dismiss it as unworthy. It was not anything that she had said or anything that she had implied, it was subtler than that, what she had not said and how she had not reacted. He could not pinpoint it properly, even to himself, but something was wrong. He was reluctant to conjecture on what it could be but there was something. He was too experienced to be mistaken. Mary Henekey was hiding something, perhaps nothing important, but something. What the hell could it be: what could a mother in a situation like this be keeping a secret?

He had reached his own house and, not bothering with

the front door, he unlatched the little gate that separated the house from the garage. As he walked to the end of the garden a cat shot out from a lavender bush. He was not proud of his garden, the grass on the tiny lawn was badly in need of cutting and the borders were overgrown.

He stood at the back fence and looked into the other back gardens. The view was obscured by an uneven line of garages and potting sheds: all he could see of the Henekey house was the window of one of the bedrooms, the curtains were drawn. How many other houses between his and the Henekeys? It was difficult to count accurately because of the odd angles at which the other gardens co-joined, but it was about fourteen. How many people in those fourteen houses? It must be somewhere between fifty and sixty, reduce that by the obviously incapable; the young, the old, the sick, reduce it again by the women, concentrate on the young and lusty males, add on the middle-aged and sly. How many men between the ages of seventeen and fifty five in those fourteen houses? About twenty, he decided: how many capable of killing Monica Henekey? Maybe all. It was very depressing.

CHAPTER
EIGHTEEN

Shenton sat in the back of his car parked at a meter on the far side of the road from the underground railway station. He had folded away the street map and although the radio had been tuned into Channel 9 to keep him in touch with events there was nothing he could do. The arrangements had been made, the watchers were in place, Inspector John Purchase was installed in the girl's room. Detective Sergeant Marilyn Cullen, complete with blonde wig, was waiting in the lobby office. The heavy mob were in the basement.

Miss Sylvia Jenkins had been taken by unmarked car two stations down the line so that she could appear at the station as if she had returned from her job in the City. Everything that could be done had been done: all that there was now to do was to wait. And all that was now necessary to ruin the whole charade was for chummy to decide to have a night off. To switch tactics, to stay at home, or even try a more likely victim, to act on impulse.

Shenton lit his pipe and let down the passenger window to allow some of the smoke to escape: the waiting was always the worst part but even worse, of course, for the girl rattling along now in the train, keyed up and wondering what she had let herself in for: wondering if he was on the train, if he would leap out as she walked up the stairs of the station. It can't be any fun that, Shenton puffed his pipe towards the roof of the car, to be a girl knowing that a sex maniac has marked you down and is waiting for you, no matter how many policemen are also waiting.

The call sign came and Shenton unhooked the receiver.

'Tango seven.'

'Gypsy Four, sir. The girl has left the train and is walking through the station entrance. There is no sign of the man. He was not on the train or in the station foyer.'

'All right.'

A frost, a bloody frost, thirty two men deployed, seven cars and God knows how much andrenalin and nervous tension was being expended. Here he was in a back street outside a suburban station with a thousand better things to do, waiting for a twenty two year old girl to make her way back to a grotty bedsitter.

The call sign bleeped again.

'Shenton!'

'Gypsy Four, sir, the girl has left the station. No one answering the man's description anywhere on the station or in the road outside. Mr Jordan says he confirms that, request instructions.'

'Proceed as planned.

So Jordan had the feeling too, but what was the point in calling it off now? A mistake to key men up and then just drop it, much better to let the charade play itself out. There was always an outside chance, remote but a chance, perhaps he came by bus and it had caught a traffic light, something incalculable, trivial, he might be running through a back street right now, trying to catch up. But no, he wouldn't do that, not this joker, if something got in his way like that, he would take it as a sign and shy away, a frightened jackal.

'All I need now is for him to do one somewhere else '

'Sir?'

Shenton had not realised that he had spoken aloud. 'Nothing.'

He looked at his watch. She ought to be well on her way by now, crossing the main road with the rest of the rush hour crowd. She wouldn't know it was for nothing, she would be clutching her parcel; trying to remember her instructions, not to stare, not to be unusual. And all the time she would be so rigid that she would forget to breathe.

'Gypsy One reporting.'

'Yes.'

'Jordan sir. There was nothing at the station.'

'I got your message, we'll carry on.'

'We've overtaken the girl, and I've just watched her cross the main road and turn into Glaston Street. There's no sign of him anywhere in the main road. We'll drive up the parallel road and cut back across the top of Glaston Street.

Selby will hand her over at the top, I'll pick him up.'

'All right.'

Shenton felt tired. It was a mistake to have come out on a jaunt like this; bad management, he ought to have approved the plan and left them to get on with it. After all he had criticised Graham for doing exactly the same thing, although he at least had achieved something. He had nailed somebody. This thing looked as though it was not even going to be a glorious failure and he was adding to it just by being here. It was always more obvious if the brass was around and there were no callers. Perhaps now was the time to end it.

Again the bleeper.

'Gypsy One.'

'Yes,' said Shenton tiredly.

'I think we've hooked him at the top of Glaston Road.' Jordan's voice was excited.

'How?'

'He was in a café, a greasy spoon place at the corner. He must have been watching the girl all the way up the street.'

'And Selby?'

'It was the hand-off point. He was watching Selby as well but Selby turned off to the right to hand over to Jenkins. It was Jenkins who saw him and hung back, stopped me driving across the junction.

'Where is he now?'

'After the girl. He's a suspicious bastard, he's stopping at all the shop windows.'

'Then stay there, do nothing to alarm him. Keep everybody back.'

'She'll be at the house soon.'

'Stay where you are until the girl's inside and he's followed. Tango Four and Tango Three?'

'Here sir.'

'Take the alternative road to the other end of the street and wait there. No one to enter the street until the clear call and then all converge. Gypsy One will wait at the southern junction until my car passes. All clear?'

'Understood.'

'Calling Bravos one and six, Purchase and Miss Cullen will use radios to receive but not transmit until man enters room. Task Force take over, all radios on receive. Task Force advise.'

'Understood.'

Shenton turned the radio switch to open reception. 'You can pull out,' he told his driver, 'move up towards the junction.'

'Right sir.' The driver also was glad of some action.

Shenton settled comfortably into his seat and relit his pipe. He looked benignly out at the bad-tempered faces of the home-going crowd. It made the hell of a difference knowing that it was not all a waste of time.

'Girl entering house,' said the metallic voice. 'Suspect now ten yards from house, has stopped, is turning to look back at the street.'

Purchase held the radio tightly to his ear, conscious of his own heavy breathing. 'Girl has shut door behind her, suspect still in street, is approaching house, has stopped, has turned back.' The bastard, thought Purchase, has he seen something? A car, a van, someone looking at him, or some instinct, some animal sense of danger. 'Suspect has turned back to the house,' came the flat tinny voice, 'now approaching the front door, looking back to the street, he's opened the door. He's gone in. Over to Task Force Two.'

Silence and then footsteps approaching the door. A girl's footsteps: the key turned in the lock and Detective Sergeant Marilyn Cullen, complete with blonde wig and parcel was there, she shut the door behind her.

'Task Force Two reporting. Suspect is going towards the stairs, all units move.'

Purchase closed the aerial of his radio. Marilyn put her mouth close to his ear. 'He came into the hall as I got to the landing.'

Purchase nodded and put his hand on her shoulder: they stood like statues.

The footsteps came softly but confidently on the landing outside and at the rapping on the door the girl started. Purchase squeezed her shoulder again and then moved softly away towards the alcove and stood before the curtain. He nodded encouragingly.

'Who is that?'

'Miss Jenkins. Is this the room of Miss Sylvia Jenkins?'

Purchase listened intently, an ordinary voice, a warm voice with a great deal of persuasion.

'Yes, Sylvia Jenkins, who is that?'

'Could I speak to you for a moment?'

Purchase cautiously moved behind the curtain into the alcove, still straining to hear the voice. 'I'm from the Ministry of Social Security, Miss Jenkins. There is a discrepancy over the stamps on your card. I won't keep you for a moment, would you open the door, please?'

Purchase went fully behind the curtain as Marilyn clicked the bolt of the door.

'What about my card?'

'I have it here, there are two stamps missing. When I saw the address, being on my way home, I thought why not call and . . .'

He's good, thought Purchase, the bastard's bloody good. He sounds relaxed.

The door clicked shut.

'You've closed the door!' Marilyn's voice had a note of hysteria to it.

'This won't take a second. It's just the card—look—'

A sharp intake of breath, a kind of strangled gasp and Purchase wrenched open the curtain. The man had her by the throat, doubled over, forcing her down. Purchase took a single step and leapt, hitting him with the point of an elbow across the side of the head. It sent the man sideways and the girl fell away somewhere to land on her knees.

Purchase had a perfect neck-hold on him now, forearm and wrist across the throat, knee in the small of the back. The man struggled like an impaled worm, elbows jabbing back, heels kicking up.

'Keep trying you shit, come on, try all you want. I'll break your bastard back.'

The door crashed back, almost unhinging itself and the room was suddenly full of policemen. Purchase pulled the man up from the floor without releasing his neck-hold and then propelled him between the first pair of the newcomers. They took him by the arms to prevent him falling.

'Did you clout him?'

'Yes.'

'And me.' Marilyn Cullen was examining the torn knees of her tights. 'As soon as he got hold of me I got my heel up him.'

'Good girl.'

Purchase grabbed a handful of the man's hair and forced the head back. He looked into the narrowed eyes. 'What's the name?'

There was no answer. Purchase wrenched open the jacket and made a quick search: there was nothing very much, a handkerchief, some loose silver, a pair of sunglasses. The inside breast pocket was closed by a zip fastener. 'A cautious bastard.' The eyes flickered and then were still. Purchase pulled the zipper and took out a notecase which he carried over to the window so that he could examine it the better. A few pound notes, one fiver, some papers, a driving licence.

There was a murmur of voices in the crowded doorway and Shenton was allowed through. He glanced at the prisoner but moved first to Marilyn Cullen.

'Are you all right?'

'Yes sir, just a torn pair of tights. He didn't have much chance to get going.'

'Well done. Do we know who he is?'

'Gordon Williams, sir, of Osterley Park.' Purchase held up the wallet. 'It needs to be checked but he had this well secured inside his jacket.'

'Then Williams it is. You've had quite a long run, Mr Williams.'

Gordon Williams said nothing, he looked slight between the two policemen who stood on either side of him. A lump was beginning to rise up on the left side of his face. He did not mind meeting Shenton's eyes but his own were expressionless. Shenton recognised the look, the shield of blankness. The eyes were intelligent enough, they moved from Shenton, to the uniformed men who were now moving round the room, once more to the girl and then again, with the only sign of curiosity, to Purchase.

'It's all over,' said Shenton. 'We'll take you down and charge you formally at the station, and then we'll check this address.'

'All right,' said Gordon Williams.

'Is there anything you want to say?'

The lips twisted in wry amusement. 'My mother's going to get the hell of a surprise.'

Milton was sitting in his bath, luxuriating at the warmth that soaked out some of the tiredness from his legs. His cigarette had burned down to within an eighth of an inch from his chin and, regretfully, he raised a damp finger to douse it and remove the remains to the edge of the soapdish. He would have to remember to get rid of that when he cleaned up the bathroom.

He went back to his reverie. There was something that was not right, a sour note in an otherwise perfect concerto. How was it that no one else seemed to have picked up that flat note? Or had it not appeared with anyone else: had it been a fluke that he had just happened along when Mary Henekey's guard was down?

Could it after all be something to do with the brother, Edward Henekey. Murder was supposed to be a family crime, in England at any rate, and in more than eighty per cent of all cases. What about having suspicions like that: to have your sixteen year old daughter murdered and to have no proof, because that would be something definite, something you could do something about, force a decision. But to have something much less tangible, a feeling, a hint maybe, a detail that nagged away in the background. Something like that would colour everything, because there was nothing that you could definitely say without feeling a monster but it still would not go away, would refuse to be forgotten.

Another definition of hell. He let his mind roam over the Henekey male line, there were only three feasible possibilities, the uncle, the father and the brother-in-law. He felt almost guilty in listing them. Edward Henekey was favourite but Shenton did not miss much—Edward would have been laundered every possible way there was and Edward did not add up. The times did not fit and it was always dangerous to make a man favourite just because he was a bastard. Jim Henekey? Well, he wasn't the type, a weak man, ineffectual, without an ounce of aggression in him. Anyone could be wound up to anything, given the circumstances, but what circumstances: take the lousiest possible motive you could think of, incest say. Milton winced, but kept to his line of thought, anything like that and he would have given himself away, he would have been in a state of nervous collapse and even if she had decided to protect him, if it had been Jim Henekey there would have been more strain to the mother. And he wouldn't have done it by picking her up at the bus stop, and then again the times were so wrong. Jim Henekey had a near perfect alibi, he had been seen by up to twenty people at various times. People who had nothing to do with his family at all, who had no possible reason to lie. As certain as anything could be it was not Jim Henekey.

Which left the brother-in-law. He was young, he was supposed to be very clever, certainly self-assertive, obviously personable. And at the same time no one seemed to know the hell of a lot about him. Could he have fancied her? She would have trusted him, would have got into his car without question. It wasn't bad for a jigsaw, the bits fitted or could be made to fit. There was only one thing wrong with it; his wife said that he was with her the whole evening. His wife was Monica's sister and she said flatly that he was with her and she should know.

The water was getting cold. He got up reluctantly and reached over to the towel rail.

'Are you still in there, Arthur?'

'I haven't gone away.'

'They've caught him, I've just heard it on the radio. They've caught him.'

'Good for Shenton.' He draped the second towel round his shoulders and opened the door.

'It's no help to the family but at least it's over. And I suppose I'm silly but I'm glad it's not a local man. It would have been dreadful if it had been someone we knew.'

'Especially someone the Henekeys knew.'

'Nothing will ever bring Monica back, but at least Mary can start to forget. Not to have people being interviewed all the time. Having everything questioned, and those newspapers.'

'It's never easy. What did they say about it, exactly?'

'That a man had been arrested and charged in connection

with the murders of several girls, the ones who had been killed in North London. That Mr Shenton had made a statement, why?'

'Nothing.' He bent over to pull the bathplug. 'I suppose Graham will be going up there.'

'To arrest him, you mean?'

'Hardly, the crime squad won't be letting him go. Graham will be up there to face him, to get him to cough.'

'But won't your Mr Shenton . . .'

'He's not mine, it's a technical thing. Graham's the local and he'll want a cough, it's a matter of book keeping.'

'You're dripping water all over the place. Move over, Arthur, I don't know what you mean about book keeping, surely all that matters is that he's been caught. Not that they'll hang him.'

'No, they won't hang him, don't let's go into that one. It's not good for my blood pressure.'

He put on his robe and went down into the hall to the telephone. He dialled the station number gambling that someone he knew was on the desk.

It was Newcombe.

'What about this bloke they've collared?'

'Gordon Williams of Osterley Park, what about him, I've never heard of him and nor have you. There's no sheet on him. All we've had is a call for Graham to go up there and he went off about half an hour ago.'

'I was curious.'

'Looks like you backed a loser, Arthur, from what I hear he's coughed for the lot.'

'For Monica?'

'I don't know the details. They caught him on the job and when they turned his drum over they found all his bits and pieces. His old lady went down with shock and had to be taken to hospital. Charles says he's coughed for the lot.'

'And Monica?'

'How the hell do I know, but it doesn't matter, does it? They reckon that whoever did one did the lot. Stop thinking about it.'

'I wish I could.'

'Well, chat your wife then. Wish I had my old woman

handy right now. Get off and try your luck, you introspec-
tive old bastard.'

Milton was left holding the dead receiver which he
replaced very slowly.

'I still say he didn't do that one,' he said to nobody.

CHAPTER
NINETEEN

Shenton lit his pipe and passed a hand across his sore eyes. It had been an exhaustingly hard night which at last was moving towards its close. The clock on the wall of the interview room showed 2.17 a.m. On the other side of the table Gordon Williams sat relaxed but alert. He had blossomed greatly during the interrogation, becoming more and more at his ease as the questions had become more searching. He had decided to talk and he liked talking. He was enjoying himself.

Jordan was also tired and with good reason. He completed the final sentence and then massaged his wrist as he slid the final page along the table to Williams. It was silent in the interview room, a slight creaking from the chairs and a rustling from the pages as Williams read through the fourteen pages of foolscap.

'What's this bit about the Australian bird struggling when I went up her?'

'You said,' Jordan consulted his note. 'Quote "I hung onto her neck until she passed out, it was only a faint because when I'd got her drawers down she came to and started to fight as I went up her. So, I finished her." Unquote.'

'Yeah.'

'Anything you don't agree with,' said Shenton patiently, 'you are entitled to alter.'

'So long as I sign?'

'We want to get it wrapped up.'

'I bet you do.'

'Of course we do,' Jordan brought the right note of jocularity into his voice, 'you've had us running around for a year and all that time you were a jump ahead of us, until tonight. Naturally we want to get it wrapped up, all neat and tidy. That's the way you like things isn't it, your diary shows that.'

'That diary,' the ulta-white teeth flashed, 'that's what's wrapped it up. You didn't case me, I did it myself. I should have burned that book, I thought about it often enough but it would have been the hell of a pity, while I was still able to go home and read it. I used to like that.'

Shenton took the pipe out of his mouth. 'I suppose it was a way of reliving it.'

'Yeah, in a way it was better than doing it for real. I could remember how it felt, the excitement. I could concentrate on the bits that I liked best. It was great, that book, as well as all the crappy things those newspapers wrote about me. I used to get a great laugh out of them. But I knew it was stupid to keep it and taking their pants. A dead give-away.'

'Why did you keep them, knowing the danger?'

'I wasn't going to get caught was I? The way I worked I didn't see how I could be; the only danger was someone seeing me going in or out of their rooms. But that had happened and it was no sweat, some old biddy who wanted to know who I was. I thought she was going to rake the girl out until I sweet talked her. I bet she had a right attack of the screamers when she found out who she'd been talking to.'

'We have her statement. She gave me a very good description of you.'

'That nosey cow would. Anyway, I still had enough start and I never did them on my own doorstep so there wasn't much chance, was there? I thought that so long as I pulled them in their own rooms I had it a hundred to one in my favour. The last thing I had in mind was some bastard leaping out from behind a curtain.'

'You've told us a lot about the ones that you killed, Gordon, but there must have been as many that you tried and never got anywhere with.'

Williams shrugged. 'I jacked in a few, sure, they didn't have a room of their own, other girls, some of them had blokes living with them. I wouldn't try, would I; I took a lot of trouble picking those birds.'

'But there were some that did not go according to plan,' Shenton persisted. 'Where you were interrupted or something else went wrong, like Monica Henekey.'

'Who's Monica Henekey?'

'The girl that you picked up at the bus stop outside the North Road tennis club.'

'Balls! I read about that. You want to hang it on me so you can clear your books. Well, hard fucking luck, I've never pulled any bird in the street.'

'I suppose it would have put you off, suddenly having her dead when all you wanted was to stop her making a fuss. Knowing she was dead wouldn't be the same thing at all.'

Williams grinned. 'That wouldn't have put me off so long as they're on their backs. It's a good try but nothing doing. Any bird I got to I had. I don't pull half-arsed capers in the street. Whoever did that bird was a stupid sod and that's not my style at all.'

'It wasn't that stupid, it was quite cleverly worked out in its way, because nobody did see you, at least not good enough to identify you or your car. But you were careful to do it in a district where you weren't known. It was a bit cheeky that but I suppose you felt like a bit of a change.'

'Look, I'm fed up with this, I don't give a brass fuck whether you believe me or not but I'm telling you I never saw her. It was a stupid cock up and it wasn't me. She wasn't done and that's not me at all and I'm finished talking about it.'

Shenton and Jordan exchanged glances.

'Is there anything else you want to add to that statement, anything you want to alter?'

'I've got to read it haven't I?' Williams pouted at Shenton. 'You've got my concentration crossed up.'

'Take your time,' said Shenton, and got up from the table.

The constable standing outside the door looked up expectantly as he came out and Shenton gently shook his head. He crossed the corridor to his own office. As he went in Graham rose from his seat at the end of the conference table.

Shenton nodded to him. 'We're there now. He wouldn't say anything at first but once we got the stuff from his house and told him his mother had been taken to hospital he wanted to talk. Once he got going he was like a dam bursting.'

'He's admitted them all?'

'He's told us about the five girls that were killed in their rooms. He's going over his statement now, with Jordan; he's taken a fancy to him.'

'And Monica?'

Shenton sat down at the head of the table. 'He's adamant that he had nothing to do with that. He got very ratty about it when I pressed it, that's why I've come out, I want him to sign that statement.'

'Does he own a car?'

'No, but he does have a driving licence.'

'Who is he?'

'An unmarried twenty-six year old Social Security clerk, who lives with his widowed mother. His father was an industrial chemist. He went to a grammar school and so far as we've been able to check he has never been in any kind of trouble before, or suffered from any kind of mental disorder.'

'So he's not mad?'

'Not under the old MacNaughton rules: he knew what he was doing all right and how the law regarded it. But these days?' Shenton shrugged. 'He'll probably be labelled as psychotic or whatever the word is that they use for people who look at everyone else as if they were on the other side of a plate glass window.'

'A bastard!'

'And a necrophiliac, with his looks and background, solid middle class, the academics will find him a Godsend. There'll be a shelf of books written about him.'

Graham looked defeated. 'He could still cough on the Henekey girl. A bit of pressure, while he's in the mood. A new face.'

'It's possible but I doubt it. When they chat like that one, what they don't say the first time round they rarely come to afterwards. Not even if you've got them sewn up with absolutely solid proof. It's closed off in their minds: they're not like ordinary crooks: they've got a weird logic all of their own. What they don't want to think about just doesn't exist for them.'

'It's worth a try.'

'Of course it is, as soon as he's signed that statement, he's all yours.'

'It's ironic, isn't it, all the work we did, the house-to-house and all the bloody paperwork; special patrols.'

'It got you Kevington.'

Graham grunted. 'Yeah, we did get that bastard.'

There was a knock at the door and Shenton shouted. Jordan came into the room. 'Here it is, sir, right down to the caution and the statement being freely given.'

Shenton took the sheets. 'All of them?'

'In lurid detail.'

'This is Mr Graham.'

Jordan held out his hand. 'You want him to clear up yours?'

'I don't see why he shouldn't.' He looked at Shenton. 'Go ahead.'

'I'll introduce you,' said Jordan, 'he's full of himself right now, like he's holding court. Hold on,' he put a coin into the automatic cigarette dispenser on the wall of the corridor, 'I told the craphound I'd get him a packet.'

They went into the interview room together and Jordan gave the nod to the uniformed man standing at the door to leave. Williams looked up at them and frowned when he saw a stranger. Graham stared hard and with some distaste, at the thick dark hair and the bushy eyebrows. There was something dark about Williams altogether, his skin had a bluish tinge to it. Under Graham's stare his eyes half closed and he took on the look of a bird of prey. He moved slightly in his chair and his frown turned to a grin as he looked at Jordan.

'Let's sit down.' Jordan pulled two chairs up to the interview table.

'First of all . . .' Graham began.

Jordan chimed in. 'Gordon doesn't mind talking, do you Gordon? He's quite a boy and he's been very co-operative.' Jordan slid his packet of cigarettes across the table and Williams picked them up and commenced, leisurely, to strip off the cellophane wrappings. He got out one of the cigarettes and Jordan lit it for him.

'All right,' he propped his elbow up on the table and regarded Graham superciliously. 'What do you want?'

'I want to know about Monica Henekey. A sixteen year old girl on the North Road, you remember.'

'Not that crap again.'

'She came out of the tennis club and you picked her up at the bus stop. You picked her up and you killed her and then you dumped her body on wasteland up by the golf course. You killed her but you didn't rape her and I want to know why.'

'You're talking balls. I've never been on any North Road.'

'Come on, why so shy, why not tell us? Did her dying so quick put you off?'

'Are you kidding?' The lips drew back on startlingly white teeth. 'Put me off, you silly bastard, it's the way I wanted them, all laid out and no complaints. That way I could do what I liked.'

'Proud of that, are you?'

Williams blew a cloud of smoke squarely into Graham's face. 'You can't upset me, copper: I've coughed it all to the fuzz here and they're going to take good care of me. They've got their little case all sewed up and no bastard from outside is going to mess it up for them. I've coughed on all the ones I did. I killed five, copper, I sorted them out, picked the ones I fancied, killed them and had them. I didn't mess about like the silly sod you're on about.'

'Why kill them?'

'Because I wanted to, because it was the way I liked it, because it's what the bloody aggravating tarts deserved. I went straight in and no messing. It don't make any difference anyway, aggravated rape with those birds telling the tale, would have got me life anyway and killing them gave me a better run. And I liked it, I enjoyed it; I enjoyed feeling them go.'

'Tell the truth about this girl, Williams!'

'Get stuffed.' He turned to Jordan. 'Get this bastard out; I'll say nothing more while he's here.'

'Righty O, then.' Jordan got to his feet and Graham followed him. They waited at the door for the constable to come back and station himself on guard and, as Graham turned for a final stare, Williams blew a smoke ring at him.

'Lousy little shit, ain't he?' said Jordan as they crossed the corridor, 'absolutely glories in it but being matey was the only way to get it out of him, that and asking him about

the bits and pieces he collected. It must have been relief or
something that we didn't laugh at him. Unless the bastard is
trying for an insanity plea. Though I don't think he cares
either way, just before he signed that statement he told me
that even if he did spend the rest of his life in the boob, he'd
still have his memories to look back on.'

'He killed that girl on the North Road all right.'

Jordan shrugged. 'If you say so, but you'll never get him
to admit it.'

Jordan knocked on the door and they went in when
Shenton called. He was still sitting at the conference table
with Williams's statement in front of him, and he laid down
his pencil as they came up to the table. He looked at
Graham's face.

'No luck?'

'No.'

'He's said more than enough about the other five.' He
handed the statement to Jordan. 'Ten photocopies for now.
Are we all right to get him for a magistrate's hearing
tomorrow?'

'They're arranging a special court for him. Ten thirty. He
says he doesn't want a solicitor tonight.'

'Then the sooner the better.'

'I'll have these photographed now. Will you want the
original, sir?'

'Not tonight, but we'll have it locked in the station safe.'

'I'll see to it.' Jordan held his hand out to Graham. 'I
hope you get a break.'

'Thanks.'

Shenton motioned Graham to the seat next to his. 'Without an admission from Williams there is absolutely nothing
to connect him with the Henekey girl.'

Graham sat heavily on the chair. 'He must have done it,
there can't be two of them within six miles of each other,
killing girls for kicks and both using the same method. I
think he's playing a game, having a laugh at getting us at it.'

Shenton pulled a scrap pad forward and engrossed himself in sketching an elaborate pattern of interlacing circles.
He did not look up for a full five minutes.

'It is always possible,' he said eventually, 'that he will
only accept responsibility for the killings that he thinks of as

successes. The Henekey girl was not violated. If there was a sexual intent then something went wrong; perhaps she tried to get out of the car and he had to kill her to keep her quiet. That way he could possibly think there was something to hide, otherwise he would have to admit that there was one in which he was unsuccessful or panicked, and that would touch his self-esteem.'

Graham nodded vigorously. 'That's what I think: it must have been him. It was the first time that he had tried it in the open and it's probably why he never did it again. The girl must have tried to attract someone's attention, got the door open, something like that and once he'd knocked her off, the last thing he'd do would be to keep her in the car. He'd dump her at the first opportunity. He panicked and he'd never confess to anything like that: it's not glamorous enough.'

Shenton laid aside his pencil. 'It could have been like that,' he said softly, 'but what do we have to support that it was?'

'No hard evidence but he didn't leave any at the scene of the other killings, did he?'

'No, but he did keep a very extensive diary, a collection of newspaper cuttings on all the acts he committed, and pieces of clothing that he took from the girls he killed. There were five pairs of girls' knickers among them: it's probably going to be impossible to match them forensically with the five girls who were killed but I'm as certain as I can be that they were taken from the five that he admits to killing. Monica's knickers were taken and if it was Williams I would expect him to hang on to them. Otherwise he would have deliberately drawn attention to the Henekey murder by making it similar to his others and then refused to admit to himself that it had anything to do with him.'

'He would have had the reaction afterwards and then got rid of them, maybe days afterwards and burnt any cuttings he'd collected about it.'

'I accept that, there is no reason why he should act consistently all the way through. But the fact remains that there is not one piece of circumstantial evidence that connects Williams with that case. The man who killed her used a car. Williams can drive a car but he does not own one. There is no evidence that he hired or borrowed one that night. He left home without one and returned without one.'

'He could have stolen it.'

'True, but in every other case he has taken very great care, fanatical care, to minimise his chances of discovery. He has spent weeks, sometimes months, checking up on his victims. In his room there was a list of eighteen girls' names that he had copied out from the Social Security records, concentrating on those who lived in multi-tenancies. He always started with the name, and only after he had the name and address would he hang about near where she lived, at the bus stop or tube station, to follow her home. He moved cautiously and with great cunning. He never spoke to any of them in the street and when he did approach them, he knew their name, their age, what they looked like; everything he could possibly know about them. He is a gloater. He delights in secret knowledge. Everything points to him not being a killer of impulse. He is a freak, absolutely out of the normal run: but, if he killed Monica then he had to be acting diametrically opposite to everything that he has done in any other case. To drive a stolen car through an area which he did not know and, on impulse, to pick up a girl he knew nothing about, to kill her in the open and then to drive on with the body in the car, completely at risk until he left the body on a wasteground. And taking another great risk to do that. And, after that to drive the car, which he had no guarantee had not been reported stolen, back to where he lived, which is over six miles away, to appear at his normal time.'

'It's out of character, I agree, sir. But for my money it's still him. It doesn't have to be a stolen car, he could have hired one, maybe days before, and left it in the street. His mother would never have known that. He could have been driving round the streets for months without doing anything. He's an isolate and they often drive aimlessly, it gives them privacy and means they can look at people from the outside.'

'We're dealing with the balance of behaviour and it must apply equally to the girl. The one certain fact we have is that Monica Henekey could not have conceivably known

Williams and she was a cautious, modest and shy girl. She never allowed herself to be picked up. If it was out of character for Williams to chance his arm in the open it is even more out of character for the girl to have got into a car with him.'

There was a long silence before Graham stirred.

'I never knew the girl and I can't explain why she should have done that either. I agree that everything we've heard about her points to her turning down someone she did not know but the fact remains that she was standing at that bus stop, a car did stop and she did jump into it in bloody quick time. I don't think we are ever going to know why. It could be that when he drew up, she took him for someone else. She was in a hurry and didn't look too closely, took it for granted and before she realised she'd made a mistake, he'd driven off. What I do know is that we've spent six weeks working on the theory that it was either someone she was related to or knew almost as well as she knew her own family. We've checked every one of them and they're all clean. We've done a house-to-house: we've checked up on anyone that she knew, half knew, ones she maybe didn't know but who knew her by sight. We've checked on every local who had the opportunity. We've checked them all and in each case we've come up with a lemon. So, we've either missed something of significance or it's a conspiracy. If it was anyone with a connection with her then it must be a conspiracy because it wouldn't only be the man himself, someone would have to be covering for him. Someone willing to tell the lies to shield him and still be willing to do that knowing what he has done. And not just lying once but to keep on doing it through all the back checking, without showing any of the pressure.'

'It still doesn't explain why the girl would have got into the car.'

'I can't explain that, except what I've already said, that she mistook him for someone else. But if we're talking about a balance of possibilities then it comes back to Williams. It must be him; I feel it. It's not just that I want to get rid of it on to him so that I can clear the books. I just cannot see that there is another man going out to knock a girl off in exactly the same way as he does just for the sake of it. And once you discount it being someone with a connection with the girl, that's what it comes to.'

Shenton nodded and then, with either a groan or a sigh, reached down to the side of his chair and brought up his document case. He drew out his file, opened it, glanced at the last two pages, and then looked up.

'I think that that is as far as we go. In the absence of any other indication, I can see no point in continuing the investigation into the Henekey girl's death as a major enquiry. I will make my report on those lines. The investigation has been exhaustive but apart from the possibility of Williams, no other worthwhile line of investigation has been uncovered. I shall recommend that the Squad be withdrawn. If anything further does come to light then, obviously, the position would need to be considered again.'

He rose from the table and Graham followed him. Shenton held out his hand. 'I have been very impressed by the degree of co-ordination: I've studied all the reports very closely and I have no criticism of any kind. I really have been most impressed: that will be in my report, and a copy of that will, of course, be sent to your Chief Constable.'

Graham looked startled and then flushed and they shook hands again.

After Graham had gone Shenton went back to the window and stood for a long time looking down into the street. Because it had been built into a corner of the building his line of vision gave him an oblique view of the cross-roads. There was no traffic and beyond the street-lamps illuminating the crossroad corners there was an utter blackness. He looked at his watch, 2.42 a.m. It had been a very long day and it was the end of a very long trail. A satisfactory day to have put away a mass murderer. There is always something dramatic about that. No wonder he felt old, it was the end of an investigation that had taken over a year of intensive effort. A classic of its kind. A year of sudden journeys, of speculation, of intense mental effort, of gambles and of broken sleep.

He was too old to be standing in the middle of the night engaging in further speculation. It was time to switch off. Tomorrow was another and very different day. A day of contemplation and also for the drawing up of his final report on the man who had roamed North London for over a year and in that report Monica Henekey would also receive her modest due. It was always tempting to close a file and what he wrote might even be true.

Williams no longer existed as a man but as a kind of dustbin. A scapegoat; a depository for the unspeakable. Shenton rubbed the back of his neck. Williams did not kill Monica Henekey and although his report would not say that he did, the fact that her name appeared in that report with the statement that no other suspects were known, a certain psychological atmosphere would be created. Assumptions would be made and his recommendation that the case no longer rated a major enquiry would certainly be accepted.

Who did kill her? There was no real answer to that question. The only honest answer would be that I, James Shenton, detective of high rank and much experience, do not believe that Monica Henekey was murdered by Gordon Williams. I do not believe it because my instincts tell me that because of the kind of girl that she was and he the kind of cold sensualist that he is, it was impossible that they would ever have met without springing apart like repelling poles. But I have no idea who it was that did murder her. I have no instinctive, even wild suspicions, and that is very rare. The only other certainty I have, based upon my well known intuition, is that I never will know who killed her, or why. It would be kinder to her family to let it go. Whoever it was he must be a very unusual man because the girl trusted him, trusted him so utterly that she did not even think about it. And he killed her. Why? Certainly for none of the usual understandable, squalid reasons. It was a mystery, a true mystery, the only truly mysterious killing that he had ever met with, and it had defeated him.

His shoulders sagged a little as he walked back to the conference table and collected up his papers. He shuffled them neatly into order and then locked them into his document case. He stood with his case in his hand for a further minute and then, with a final shrug, he went across to the cupboard to collect his hat and coat.

CHAPTER
TWENTY

For the first time in weeks Milton found himself able to drive his car into his usual parking space. The area behind the station had an unusually tidy appearance: the jumble of squad cars had gone and the trailer van, that had been used as a mobile headquarters, had been towed away to its storage position at the back of the station garages.

He entered the station by the yard entrance and was immediately hemmed in by stacked cartons. As he went further along the corridor there were desks and chairs stacked against the walls and then two cadets loading up a trolley with box files under the supervision of Sergeant Charles.

'It's over then.'

Charles lifted an eyebrow. 'Sorry to see us go?'

'It's been interesting, cramped but educational.'

'Like a broken arm.'

'What'll happen to this lot?'

Charles shrugged. 'Junked, there's no point in keeping it. It would make a few bob as waste paper but orders are orders and they'll be shredded or burned.'

'It was all a waste then.'

'If you like. They'd never have got him through this lot but it seemed like a good idea at the time, to someone. Shenton's a lucky bastard, if he don't cop them one way they fall in his lap another.'

'Always?'

'Since he's run this squad he's had them all. He had a sweat on this one though, more than a year. I bet he was beginning to wonder.'

'What's your next one?'

'No idea. I'll send you a card.'

'You do that, good luck.'

'And you.'

The CID room had returned to roughly normal: his desk had been pulled back from the wall and he heaved it round so that he once more faced the door. A wad of crime reports had been thrown into the in-tray and he flipped through

them with an inward sigh. Three schools had been vandalised in as many nights and obscenities had been scrawled
across the main window of the supermarket next to the
billiard hall: the aerosol paint bandit strikes again! Seven
complaints of damage to their cars from patrons of the El
Hombre supper club who had emerged around midnight to
discover headlamps smashed and bodywork pitted by airgun pellets. A man was posing as a council inspector and
conning old age pensioners out of their rates money.

The door crashed back to admit Sheehan, huge and
awkward. 'You look bloody terrible,' Milton told him.

Sheehan rubbed a reflective hand across his chin. 'It's not
that bad, is it? I didn't get to kip until five.'

'Why?'

'I took Chris up West. We went with a mate of hers and
her boyfriend, Jimmy Cole, good bloke, runs his own
plumbing business, knows the hell of a lot of clubs.'

'Hardly worth going to bed.'

'We got back around three but we had to sit around until
the other two pushed off.'

'I see.'

Sheehan looked as abashed as he was ever likely to. 'Is
there a new rota? I've got a hell of a lot of rest days owing.'

'So have I, we'll get it sorted out this morning. How is
Chris?'

'She's great, fine.'

'You'd better read these,' Milton tossed over the crime
reports, 'it'll get your blood pressure down.'

The telephone rang and it was Durant wanting Milton.

'If he's sorting rest days, Skip, I'd like next Friday off.
This bloke Cole has got some tickets for the International at
Wembley.'

'That's OK by me.'

Durant was sitting forward in his chair studying a large
piece of graph paper that he had carefully inscribed in
various coloured inks.

'As you know, the major enquiry has ended so we can get
back to normal. A lot has been let slide these past weeks
and it needs getting a grip of: you've read last night's crime
sheets?'

'Yes, sir.'

'I want something done about those vandalised cars.'

'It's a bit difficult.' Milton kept a straight face. 'Nothing was stolen; a panda car might do it.'

'I've arranged for a special patrol but you go up there. There's a council estate round the corner from that club. Get up there and put the fear of God into them.'

'Yes, sir.'

'We go back to normal duty turns as from today. No one books overtime without my authority. Both you and Sheehan have five rest days due but I don't want more than one taken at a time.'

'I know Sheehan wants next Friday. I don't mind fitting in with him.'

'All right.' Durant picked up his green ball point pen and made a tiny alteration to his graph. 'Sheehan can have next Friday and you take the first of yours tomorrow. I want something done about those cars before then.'

'You want me to give the cars first priority, sir?'

Durant sat back in his chair and arched his fingers precisely together. 'Do you know Councillor Holmes, Milton?'

'I know he's on the Watch Committee, sir.'

'He is a member of that supper club.'

'And his car—. . .'

'No, and it's not going to be.'

'It's only kids.'

'Then it should be easy to stop them.' He gave his usual abrupt gesture of dismissal and Milton left.

He returned to the CID room to find that Sheehan had left in response to a call from a supermarket which had caught a thief. He scribbled a note on Sheehan's pad about his rest day and returned to his own desk. Before he could sit down the telephone rang again. The manager of a building firm wanted to talk to the crime prevention officer. Milton waved two fingers into the air and then opened his notebook and wrote down the address. He promised to call around four.

The crime reports had to be gone through again and then he remembered that he had to make his final report on the list that Graham had given him. Nothing but bloody paperwork. Temporary Detective Constable Reed returned from his investigations into the theft of forty eight lengths of copper piping which a jobbing plumber had kept in his back garden.

'Asking for it, Skip, the bloody garden backs onto a sports field.'

'No fence?'

'Yeah, two feet high.'

He got rid of the chore of returning the heap of CRO files onto Reed and pecked out his report to Graham on the old typewriter. It was already noon and the trivia was still only half sorted. Another telephone call, this time from Happy Harry, with yet another of his farcical loads of old mooley about a bank raid.

'Leave off, Harry.'

'But I heard them, Mr Milton, five of them there were, real hard cases; they'll have shooters and all.'

'Where?'

'In the second bar at The Bell, they had a map, you know, working out where to switch cars and all that. I didn't recognise them but I could do a picture for you, one of those Photofit things. They'll have records all right, right ugly mob they are, they'll have form as long as your arm.'

'And, of course, they didn't mind talking about all this right in front of you.'

'They had their back to me, Mr Milton. I sat there quiet like a mouse, never looked at them. Big-headed lot they are.'

Milton sighed. 'What did you watch on the telly last night Harry?'

'Telly? Bloody telly, now listen, Mr Milton . . .'

'Goodbye Harry.'

He passed over to Reed the names of the old dears who had given their money to the wrong man, which left the school vandals—nothing much to be done there. Nothing much to be done on the busted headlights outside the supper club either, but he'd still have to go up to the council estate and then there was that other thing, the factory that wanted a crime prevention visit way over on the other side of the High Street, but he ought to be able to make it to the council estate first. That way it ought to be an early night, so long as some silly bastard didn't do anything stupid, like make Happy Harry's dreams come true.

The telephone rang again.

'Yes?' he said, warily.

'Arthur?' came his wife's voice. 'Mary's asked if I could sit with Judith this evening, you won't be in until late, will you?'

'I was trying to make it early tonight.'

'Oh I'm sorry, I've already said that I would. I didn't know you were going to be in, you've been out so much, lately.'

'It's all right, I'll have a drink with someone.'

'There are only sausages, I forgot about the shopping until it was too late.'

'I like sausages.'

'I'll put them in the oven. I'll get you some steak tomorrow.'

'Good, don't worry, I'll sort myself out. Give Mary my love.'

He shuffled the papers of his final report on Graham's list and lit a cigarette. He went through his notebook and came across the notes he had made when he made his rounds of the doctors, how long ago? Too long ago. His wife was right, it didn't help. Who could really care what happened in some other place to people you had never seen? All that really mattered was what happened in the place that you were. And the way they were was that someone had killed Monica Henekey and Monica was real, she wasn't a statistic or something in a newspaper. We knew her and that makes it very different. Why did they kill her? Maybe because they wanted to rape her but lost their nerve. Maybe. Or maybe it was nothing to do with that but just because they were jealous of her. Because she was young and beautiful and unspoiled and everything that they were not. There were people like that as well. There are all kinds of people.

He stubbed his cigarette and got up, searching for his car keys. Reed looked up from his share of the crime sheets.

'Anything on, Skip?'

'I'll be up at the council estate on the other side of the High Road.'

'Something special?'

'A gunman.' He grinned at the expression on Reed's face. 'A kid with an airgun who doesn't like rich bastards.'

'He's not the only one.'

CHAPTER
TWENTY ONE

It was in the late evening as Milton was walking from the main road to his own home that he became aware of the man walking ahead of him. It was the unsteadiness of the man's gait that he first noticed: it was not until he was less than a dozen feet behind him that he recognised the man.

Jim Henekey had never been a particularly robust figure. Although more than six feet tall he had always been slimly built, and in his middle age there was still something boyish about him. But now the head was down and the shoulders so dramatically stooped that the back of the jacket had pulled up more than six inches from its true line. He swayed as he walked, swerving to the edge of the pavement and back again, like a drunken collier.

Milton increased his pace until he had drawn level.

'Hello, Jim.'

The head came abruptly erect and, by Christ, what a mess: the mouth hung open, the abundant hair with its distinguished powdering of white at the temples was now a tangled mess, bluntly streaked with grey as if it had been done with a distemper brush. The eyes were bloodshot slits sunk deeply into sockets that were the colour of cigarette ash.

Milton got his cigarettes out of his pocket. 'Have a smoke?'

'Yes,' He coughed as soon as the match was applied.

'I was just going in,' said Milton. 'But there won't be anyone there, my wife's round your place.'

'Yes,' said Henekey again: his eyes were watering from the cigarette which he had left hanging, inexpertly, from the corner of his mouth. He had shaved very badly.

'I feel like some company. What about coming in for a drink? If there's a pack of women round your place you can feel out of it. I know I do.'

He held Henekey's arm and guided him through the garden gate and up the shallow step onto the porch. He held onto him while he found the key and then had to help him into the hall. Henekey was going fast by the time he got him into the lounge and onto the settee.

'You look a bit done in, Jim.'

'Headache—'s a headache.'

'Let's get that jacket off.' As Milton manipulated the arms he felt the pulse rate, it was very sluggish.

'Come on then, Jim boy, what have you been up to?'

'Home, got to go home.'

'In a minute, I'll help you round there.' Milton went rapidly through the jacket pockets and found the bottle and angled it up to the window to read the label—Sodium Amatyl.

'How many of these pills did you take, Jim?'

'Alone, leave me alone.'

Milton took his pulse again, it was slow but no slower than before and it was still regular. Milton sighed and took off his jacket and tie: he pulled Henekey to his feet but he couldn't stand him up, the legs kept giving way. It was the hell of a struggle to settle him across his shoulders and going up the stairs was worse, Henekey was so long that his legs dragged across each step. In the bathroom he had to let him go, the endless, floppy legs, skidding seven different ways, kicking up the bathmat and knocking over the stool. Milton wrenched the collar open and then turned the head round and over the lavatory basin.

'Come on, Jim boy, it'll be over soon and you'll feel the hell of a lot better.'

'Ugh!'

Milton got the mouth open and his thumb on the back of the tongue. Henekey began to struggle and Milton had to hold him down with his knees while he used both hands to hold the mouth open. Henekey squirmed and wriggled, trying to heave himself upwards, but there was little that he could do and then he retched and all the fight went out of him. Milton laid him back gently on the floor, found a towel, soaked it in cold water and wiped the sweat away from Henekey's face and neck. He rolled up the bathmat and put it under the head before he went downstairs again.

The only doctor he could think of was Godfrey and his surgery was closed with the calls switched through to an answering service. Milton found the private number and obviously interrupted something.

'I'm sorry about it but I don't want to make this official or cart the poor bastard off to hospital. I don't know how many pills this bottle would hold, it's about an inch high and there are ten or so left. If he'd meant to do himself in he'd have taken the lot. I reckon he's taken them to dull things, or maybe he was confused.'

'You should still get him to hospital, to cover your-self.'

'I know, but how many times do you kick someone in the face? If I have him up there they'll keep him under observa-tion a couple of days at least and that will knock the hell out of him. I want to know how serious it is.'

'No doctor in this situation would hand a man in that state enough for him to end his life. That size of bottle is a standard week's supply, he'll be on three, so he shouldn't have been able to have taken more than twenty at the outside. It would make him ill and lose co-ordination but it's not likely to be fatal, but this is all conjecture, he could have taken something else as well.'

'He was at his worst when I found him in the street, since then I've made him spew up and his pulse is much steadier, it's still slow but it's regular.'

'Then it looks all right but this is very unfair, Arthur, I don't know the man's full history, he's not my patient and you are not a doctor. I cannot possibly make a diagnosis over the telephone.'

'I know, but you've instructed me to get him to hospital, haven't you? It's all down to me now.'

'I should get an ambulance round there myself.'

'But I've said I'll do that.'

'Have you?'

'Just now, didn't you hear me?'

Godfrey gave some kind of groan. 'You take some bloody terrible chances, Arthur.'

'All the time. But thanks for putting me straight, you can get back to your game of ludo.'

After he had replaced the telephone he went out into the

kitchen and found the coffee pot and then back into the sitting room for the whisky which he finally discovered at the back of the sideboard cupboard. When he took the coffee and whisky upstairs again Henekey was still on the bathroom floor, he was breathing more easily and seemed asleep but he stirred as Milton knelt beside him and held the whisky against his teeth. 'Just a sip: to wash that taste out of your mouth.'

Henekey opened his eyes with a great effort and took some of the coffee which almost immediately dribbled out of the corner of his mouth again. Milton got his arm around his back.

'Come on Jim, sit up, you're looking better already. How many of those pills did you take?'

'Leave me alone.'

'I can't let you sleep just yet. There's ten pills left in that bottle, how many did you take?'

'Get off.'

'Don't be stupid, I ought to have you in hospital by rights, making them pump your stomach out and we don't want any of that, do we? You and Mary have had enough without more doctors and officials and police.'

'You're a bloody copper.'

'Right now I'm the bloke who lives round the corner.'

'I want to go home.'

'All right then, get up on your feet.'

Henekey made a valiant effort, he made it to his knees and then got upright by clinging onto the door frame. 'I feel bloody terrible.'

'How many pills, Jim?'

'Eight or nine, is that whisky?'

'I thought of giving you some but it reacts against barbiturates.'

'I can't have much of them left after what you did. I want to wash.'

'Sure, you want any help?'

'I'm all right.' He stumbled across to the washbasin and started to run the cold water. Milton turned the bathstool the right way up and sat down; while Henekey put his head under the tap he uncorked the whisky bottle and gave himself a thoughtful drink. Some early night. He handed up the towel from the floor when Henekey came spluttering from the handbasin.

'Better?'

'A bit, where's my jacket?'

'Downstairs, I'll give you a hand.'

'For Christ's sake, stop grabbing hold of me.'

Milton watched him get to the door and then followed him down the stairs with one hand up against the wall and the other on the banisters, something was working at last, some spark, aggression or whatever, was making the adrenalin flow. By the time Henekey reached the bottom of the stairs he was able to walk more or less normally into the lounge.

'A big improvement,' said Milton, 'you can have that drink now if you want it.'

'I want to get home.'

'Sit down for a minute, every little helps. You sure you don't want one, a small one? I am.'

'I suppose you thought—that I'd—I was—'

'All I know is that you were weaving around the pavement. I don't think you were meaning to do yourself in, you'd have made a better job of it if you had. You just wanted to get home, that's why you were in this road.'

'Yes—I could feel—'

'Where were you when it started?'

'In the park, I was sitting in the park.'

'And you felt depressed so you took a few more tranquillisers than you ought to have done. It could happen to anybody.'

Henekey was searching his pockets. 'I had some cigarettes.'

'Help yourself.' Milton tossed his packet onto the coffee table and poured out a couple of small whiskies.

'You know, Jim, I never came round to see you because you'll have had more than enough people calling round and I know that words aren't any good anyway. No one can say any damn thing that means anything. Here, try this, it could do you a bit of good.'

Henekey drank his whisky too quickly and began to choke.

'Just tell me to shut up if you want to. All I wanted to say was that I remember Monica from the time that she was a little girl. That I used to envy you being her father because I was never lucky enough to have any children of my own. I still envy you because you were her father with all the agony and torment that you are going through now because you did have her for those sixteen years. They were golden years the like that I will never have.'

Henekey wept copiously, the tears coming down his face until they dripped from the end of his chin.

Milton got up and carried the whisky bottle across to him, the glass had fallen down between Henekey's knees and Milton retrieved it with difficulty: he poured some more of the whisky and held it up to the wet lips. He had to put his arm around Henekey's head to hold it steady.

'Come on now boy, drink up, just let yourself go, it's better than pills.'

Henekey took the whisky and then another; he looked up at Milton through streaming eyes. 'I loved her.'

'I know.'

'I loved both of them and now—'

'Hold it steady.' The whisky was splashing over both his hand and Henekey's chin.

'—both of them. I've lost both of them.' He was drinking the whisky almost greedily now, and then suddenly he convulsed sideways, almost dislocating Milton's right shoulder.

'Nothing,' it was almost a whisper. 'I've nothing now, nothing at all.'

Milton manoeuvred him round so that he could lay him full length along the divan. He put a couple of cushions under his head and then laid the jacket across the shoulders. He went back to his own chair and salvaged himself a drink from the dregs of the whisky bottle. The front of his shirt was drenched with sweat and he wrenched open his collar before he lit a cigarette.

What the Christ had that last bit been about? He felt a sickening apprehension that a door was opening into an unknown room, forcing him to look at something that he did not wish to see. Both of them?

I loved both of them, he had said, I've lost both of them and now there is nothing. Milton finished his whisky and upended the bottle for the final dregs. So what do I do now? Sweet Christ, all I wanted to do was to get the poor bastard off the street so that he did not collapse into the gutter, or maybe get to his own house and fall over the step and start up the whole ponderous machine again, of men in uniform and ambulances and form filling. To allow him to keep a bit of dignity: to do what is laughingly called a neighbourly act.

Whichever bastard it was who said that nothing is ever really what it seems to be sure knew what he was talking about. If I ring up Graham what do I tell him? And if he drags Shenton back into it all? What does it mean, another turning over, endless questions, another go through the wringer? And did Jim Henekey really kill his own daughter? Was it possible?

'Of course it's possible,' Milton spoke to the ceiling. Anything is possible. He felt a little light headed and there was a lot of sweat on his forehead. What the hell is wrong with me, I haven't drunk that much? Lots of fathers have killed their children, we all know that, murder is a family crime. But *Jim Henekey*?

A moan came from the divan and he looked across at the lanky form draped across its length. You poor, unlucky bastard, whatever it means, you've lost all right. It wasn't only Monica who got killed that night.

He got up from his chair with an effort and went out into the hall, carefully closing the door behind him. He took the telephone from its stand and sat with it on the stairs hesitating for some time before he dialled the number.

It was his wife who answered. 'Is something wrong, Arthur?'

'No, but I've got Jim here and I thought I'd ring up in case Mary was wondering where he was. Is she there?'

'She's upstairs with Judith. Is Jim all right?'

'He's tired, he fell asleep in our sitting room and I've left him there.'

'Poor man, hold on Arthur, Mary's coming down.' There was a muffled conversation and then Mary Henekey came on the phone.

'What's the matter with him?' There was a very sharp note to her voice.

'He's asleep, I didn't want you to worry about him.'

'Why did he come to your house?'

'I met him in the street and we came here, we've had a few drinks, talked for a bit and . . .'

'He was talking?'

'Yes. Look Mary,' Milton lowered his voice and strained his ears towards the living room door, 'he was a bit rambling, he'd taken a couple of pills that the doctor had given him but there's nothing to worry about. I brought him in for a chat but after a bit he said he was tired and . . .'

'How many pills?'

'Not many, there is absolutely nothing for you to worry about.'

'Can he walk?'

'Of course he can walk. I thought you'd like to know where he was. I didn't mean to frighten you. I'll let him have his sleep out and it doesn't matter if he stays here the night.'

'No,' there was a distinctly ugly edge to the voice now. 'If he can walk he can come home.'

'You mean now?'

'Yes, tell him to come now.'

'Well, all right, I'll tell him.' He replaced the telephone.

Curiouser and curiouser. So Mary Henekey did not give a damn about whether her husband was ill or not but she did greatly resent him being off the lead.

When he went into the dining room and switched on the light, Henekey was staring up at him from the divan: blank eyes from which it was impossible to tell whether he had heard anything or not.

'How do you feel?'

Henekey grunted and then turned his head away; his face was paler even than when he had collapsed on the bathoom floor.

'I've just been talking to Mary on the phone.'

'Ugh.'

'My wife's round at your place and while I was speaking to her I mentioned that you were here, naturally.'

'Yes.' Henekey swung his legs onto the ground and sat with his head in his hands for a moment or so; the wisps of grey hair that dropped from the centre of his hairline were stuck to his forehead.

'What about some coffee?'

'I'm all right.' He shivered and Milton could see that his shirt was soaked with sweat.

'Take it easy.'

'I said I was all right.' He got up from the divan and threw aside the blanket. 'I want to go upstairs.'

Milton found his cigarettes on the floor and lit one. The room had a fusty smell to it and he opened one of the windows, the night air cutting across his throat. Then he folded the blanket over the back of one of the armchairs and straightened the cushions on the divan. In the hall he stood at the bottom of the stairs and listened to the sound of running water in the bathroom. He went out into the kitchen, where a knife and fork had been arranged on the kitchen table. The oven of the cooker was on and he opened the door to see the supper that he was supposed to have eaten. He switched off the cooker and got the oven glove to lift out the plate and put it on the draining board. At the back of the larder he found the miniature bottle of brandy that his wife had bought for the Christmas pudding that she had never made. He poured it into one of the water glasses and sat down at the kitchen table to light yet another cigarette.

He went out into the hall when he heard Henekey coming down the stairs. His face was dough white but his hair was combed flat and his eyes had more animation. He had replaced his tie. .

'I'm going,' he said shortly.

'I'll stroll round with you.'

'It's only round the corner.'

'It's no trouble.' Milton reached for his coat.

'I said I was all right, leave me alone.'

Henekey said nothing further, he had reached the final stair and continued on up the hall, opened the front door and went through it. He did not look back.

Milton shut the front door and went back to his brandy in the kitchen. It was getting too bloody complicated. Jim Henekey was walking about like a zombie, or alternatively like a man who had killed his own daughter and was carrying a particular kind of hell within himself. His wife sounded as if she hated the sight of him and just to underline it all in spades, their daughter was about to drop a baby into the world at any moment. And I'm sitting here trying to make up my mind on what, if anything, I'm supposed to do. Christ, I feel guilty just knowing about it.

He was still sitting at the kitchen table when his wife bustled in.

'Have you had your supper, Arthur?'

'I didn't get round to it but it doesn't matter,· I got something up at the canteen.'

'You look tired.'

'It's not been a restful evening.'

'Poor Jim, he came in as I was leaving. I'm sure he's ill, so pale and weak looking: I don't think he should be out on his own.'

'I said I'd walk him back but he didn't want me to.'

'He probably just wanted to be on his own. He didn't say anything to me, just walked straight past me and up the stairs. He didn't say anything to anybody. Are you finished down here?'

Milton drained off the rest of the brandy. 'I'm finished and I'm looking forward to my bed.' He checked that the door into the garden was locked. 'She sounded a bit sharp on the phone.'

'Mary is strung up, it's easy to say things that you don't mean when you are like that, and Jim's no match for her when she's like that. She's the much stronger character.'

'They had a row?'

'They had some words, I don't really know, I was up with Judy at the time, poor girl, her baby is due any moment now. All I could do was rub her back for her. They were downstairs and then Jim went out. No, it wasn't a row, just a few words. They've been together in that house for weeks now, ever since it happened, they're both on edge. They must remind each other of so many things.'

The bolt was home on the front door and he waited for his wife to ascend the stairs before he switched off the hall light. He climbed the stairs wearily. The Henekeys had had words and Jim Henekey had walked out, he hadn't gone far but he had meant to, as far as a bottle of pills could take him.

His wife was sitting at her dressing mirror. 'The pity of it is the effect on Judith, it upsets her and it's such a shame. It should be the most beautiful moment of her life and nothing's going right, her husband can't be here, Monica, and now her parents. I feel so sorry for her.'

'Yes, it's a pity.'

'It's your rest day tomorrow, Arthur.'

'I told you.'

'Can you change it?'

'What are you on about?'

'I forgot about it. I didn't think and . . .'

'Don't look so nervous, what are you leading up to?'

'It's just that Judy . . .'

'Not again.'

'I said I would go round to stay with her at lunchtime if nothing had happened by then. I said I would, I can't let her down. It could happen at any time. It's the least I can do.'

'Her parents are there.'

'Jim's no good, she wants a woman with her and Mary can't be there, not from midday, she's got to go somewhere. I'm sorry, Arthur.'

'No, it's all right, you should stay with her. Don't worry about me.'

'But I do worry about you. You're no good at looking after yourself and if I'm not here all you'll do is to go up to some pub again. Those pies and things, you know that they don't do you any good. You eat enough rubbish as it is and when you're home I . . .'

'Don't worry about it. I've eaten the stuff for twenty years, so one more day isn't going to make any difference. I'll be able to amuse myself all right. You go and see what you can do for Judy, you're quite right, she must have someone to look out for her. And if you're not there you'll only spend the day wondering what's happening. If it's as near as all that, though, I can't understand Mary leaving her. Where is she off to?'

'To a hospital, to see someone who's very ill. I don't know who it is, at least Judy said but I've forgotten. I don't think Mary wants to go, it could be what they had the argument about but anyway he's very ill and particularly wants to see her.'

'A man?'

'A friend of theirs, yes, I remember now, someone they used to work with. Jim or Mary, or was it both of them?'

His wife had finished at the dressing table and was now fussing with something at the wardrobe. Milton sat down on the edge of the bed and took off his shoes. There was a curious abstraction about his thoughts; although they were now crowding together at great speed, at the same time he seemed to be a great distance from them. He had had a few drinks but he was nowhere near to being drunk, so why was his mind clicking around like a roulette wheel? And why was he seeing Jim Henekey's face so clearly, with those terrible, defeated eyes and that hoarse voice?

'Are you sure you don't mind, Arthur?'

'I told you.'

Unbidden, Mary Henekey's face came into his mind and the expression in her eyes as he had spoken to her when she had stood in her garden, and the tiny relief that she had shown when he had told her that there was no progress. It was strange that she had been there, in her garden, as he had walked up the road. He had been coming back from Broad Walk and—Broad Walk? The thoughts crowded one another and Milton sat motionless on the edge of the bed holding one shoe in his hand, until the final thought struck him with the force of a steam hammer.

'Christ all Bloody Mighty!'

'Arthur, what on earth's the matter?'

He looked blankly into his wife's anxious face.

'What is it, what's happened?'

'It's nothing, I'm sorry.'

'Have you got a pain? Where is it?'

'No—yes—it's gone. I'm sorry I shouted, it's all right now.'

'Where, in your stomach again?'

'No, it's not an ulcer, it was a sort of cramp, I must have twisted. I'm all right now. I don't want anything.'

'You frightened me.'

'I know I did, I'm sorry.'

He remained where he was until his wife disappeared into the bathroom and then he went to the bedroom window and pulled back the curtains. No, he couldn't see anything from here, the angle was all wrong, at least five houses blocked any view of the Henekey's house. He lit a cigarette and lay back on the bed smoking it until his wife returned.

'Who's taking Mary to this hospital tomorrow?'

'I've no idea, Jim I suppose.'

'I doubt he's well enough. I'll take her.'

'Why?'

'I may as well. I've nothing special on and it's a neighbourly sort of thing to do, isn't it?'

'It's not like you. Won't you be bored? You don't even know the man.'

'I've got a bloody good idea.'

'What?'

'Nothing.' Milton got off the bed and stubbed out his cigarette. 'Have you finished in the bathroom?'

CHAPTER
TWENTY TWO

Milton awoke late with a sick headache and the fragmented memory of a very unpleasant dream. He could not remember what it was about but he had sweated and the taste in his throat was nauseous. He got out of bed and pulled back the curtains, the dampness on the pavements was rapidly disappearing and there was the promise of a fresh, dry day without any oppressive humidity.

He could hear his wife moving about downstairs as he went across the head of the stairs to the bathroom. He found the Alka-Seltzers in the medicine cabinet and a couple of them took most of the acidity out of his mouth. He filled the handbasin with cold water and then plunged his head into it: and that helped as well. He then filled the basin again from the hot tap and got out his old twist razor and put in a new blade. Electric razors were all right but Milton never felt that he was clean without the ritual of soap and water. He shaved very carefully taking his time and by the end of it he felt ready to face the day. He knew what he had to do, it was not going to be easy, but it was something he had to do. Not for the law, not even for justice, whatever that might mean, but for himself. Why for himself? Because he was a nosy bastard.

He selected a clean shirt from the linen drawer and opened up the wardrobe, ignored the two suits he wore on the job and finally decided on dark brown linen trousers and the windbreaker that he had bought when he had thought he might try to play golf. He had been told many times that no matter what he wore he still looked like a working jack but this lot should at least show that he was trying.

'Arthur! Are you awake?'

'What's up now?'

'She's started, Arthur, the midwife's on her way, she ought to be there by now. I'll go.'

'Hold on, I'll take you.'

'It's only round the corner.'

'It'll still be quicker, I'm using the car anyway. You get your stuff together while I get it out.'

His wife searched through her bag and decided that she did not have enough handkerchiefs. As she went up the stairs again Milton moved across the hall to the front door, he opened up the garage and started up the car, pulling it out to the road. He left the engine idling while he wiped over the windscreen and then cleared out the old cigarette packets and clip board of crime sheets that had scattered themselves across the back seat. His wife came out of the front door, holding the hat on top of her head with one hand and loaded down by an enormous basket that looked as if it was holding enough to resist a minor seige, she also held the bunch of roses that she had cut from the garden.

'You don't mind do you, Arthur? It seems appropriate.'

'It's a nice idea.'

He let up the clutch, accelerated up to the corner, spun the wheel as he changed down and then drew neatly up to the kerb outside the Henekey home. He got out and went round the car to help his wife with the basket: Mary Henekey opened the front door before they reached it. She was wearing the black tailored suit that suited her so well but lightened by a scarlet shirt and chiffon scarf held at her throat by an antique choker ring. Her thick hair had been neatly dressed but her face had lost some of its healthy sheen and her eyes were dulled: she did not look as though she had slept much. His wife and Mary Henekey went upstairs together and he remained in the hall, pushing the door behind him without allowing it to catch on the latch. The door of the sitting room was open and he went across to the threshold and looked in: there was no one there, only a raincoat thrown over the back of one of the armchairs with a pair of woman's gloves lying on top of them. Someone had been doing the housework, the vacuum cleaner was still outside the broom cupboard next to the open kitchen door.

He turned back toward the stairs as he heard Mary Henekey coming down the stairs. She was startled to see that he was still in the house and she made an effort to smile.

'Margaret's a brick to keep putting up with us.'

'She likes it, when the kid's actually here you'll have to nail up the door to keep her out.'

'I don't know what we'd have done without her.'

'How is Jim?' Milton asked.

She avoided his eye. 'All right, he's better, still depressed. I've sent him up to see the doctor, but there's nothing he can do for him really, he needs something to do. I hope the doctor will send him back to work. It would be the best thing.'

'You're probably right.'

'Thank you for looking after him last night. It was very good of you. We impose on you and Margaret far too much.'

'It's nothing, are you off now?'

'Yes, I promised, otherwise—I feel so guilty about not being here but—. . .'

'She's in good hands and it could go on for hours. She'll probably still be at it when you get back. Which hospital is it you're going to?'

'Oh it's not—it's a nursing home.'

'Which one?'

'Cressley, you wouldn't know it.'

'I know it, the other side of Mannering Park, it's only six miles away, I'll drive you.'

'No.'

'Yes I will, it'll be much quicker.'

'I can't, I won't.'

'I'm going that way, I'll drop you off at Mannering Park. It's no trouble. I'm at a loose end anyway. Get your coat.'

She went reluctantly across to the living room to pick up her coat and gloves and came back into the hall even more slowly. Milton pulled the front door wide open, took the coat from her and held it out for her to get into.

She said nothing as they walked down the path to the car. He opened the door for her and ushered her into the car. He looked at her as he settled himself into the driving seat but she stared steadily ahead through the windscreen. He fired the engine and drove deliberately across the cross-

roads at the top of the street so that he could continue
directly ahead and turn into the North Road. He glanced at
her as they came level with the tennis club but she did not
turn her head, the muscles of her neck were rigid and when
he glanced down, the fingers had tightened around the
gloves lying in her lap and twisted violently. He drove on
filtering into the traffic that was turning out of the railway
station and then over the High Road and into the maze of
streets that led him out onto the arterial road and the road
west.

He took out his cigarettes and held them against the
wheel as he opened the packet. He offered them to her but
she shook her head and he held up the packet against his
mouth so that he could take one with his teeth. All the time
he watched her from the corner of his eye, waiting for her
glance, some movement of her head, a reaction however
it came that would give him an opportunity to begin,
but she did not look at him. He found his lighter and
checked the speed of the car as he put the flame against the
cigarette.

'I can park the car at Mannering Park and you can walk
through it to the nursing home. It'll give you a chance to
quieten down. You don't want to see him all tensed up like
that.'

She looked at him for the first time, a startled jerk and
then back again. Her voice was thick. 'I'm all right.'

'You're as tight as a banjo string, you've held it in too
long and now you're frightened that it's all going to collapse. You're frightened you're going to let it out, not
especially to me but to anyone. You've already said something, haven't you, or half said it, to Jim?'

'Jim?' She was looking at him now all right, with large
frightened eyes.

'He said nothing, he was incoherent. He didn't even
know where he was and after I'd got out the muck that he'd
tried to kill himself with he wanted to get as far away from
me as possible, just as you do right now, in case he did say
something. But he didn't, not a thing. All I knew was that
he had tried to kill himself.'

'No.'

'Oh yes, that's why he took those pills. I don't know if

they were enough to kill him but that's what he was trying to do all right.'

She pulled down the lever to open the car door and Milton had to lean across to hold her arm. The car swerved abruptly across the central white line and an oncoming lorry thirty yards off hooted and flashed. 'Don't be bloody silly.'

'Let me out.'

'I said I'd take you there and that's what I'm going to do.'

'I'll jump.'

'Don't get dramatic. I'm not here to goad you or cross you up more than you are already. You're on a hairline, if you don't get rid of some of that tension it will break you to pieces. You've got to get rid of it, some of it anyway. You'll always remember but you've got another daughter. She's worth something as well, isn't she? Are you going to destroy her as well?'

They drove in silence.

'Why should I be badgered by you?' She had recovered some of her calmness, an icy calm full of hatred. 'What are you anyway, a pryer, a peeper into other people's lives? Are you proud of that?'

'I'm not proud.'

'Pretending to be a friend, wheedling, eavesdropping, trying your slimy, rotten little tricks. What for, so that you can be a sergeant? That's not much to be, is it?'

'No,' said Milton, 'It's not much.'

'I don't like policemen. I never have, it's why I've never liked you. There's something creepy about you, always watching, always there, always appearing.'

'You've got nothing to fear from the police. They've packed up and gone. No one has sent me to worm anything out of you, or to set any little trap. I'm not here because I'm a policeman. I'm here because I live round the corner, because I know you and because I get curious about things. I wonder about them and after a while they fall into a pattern. It doesn't do me any good, like you say I'm a sergeant and after twenty three years of trying that is not much to be. The reason I'm here is simple, you have it festering inside you and it's either going to send you off your head or you are going to kill yourself. It's one thing or the other and that means it's got to come out.'

'I'm telling you nothing. There's nothing to know.'

He had reached the part of the road that he wanted, dual carriage with plenty of fast traffic and a deserted lay-by. He pulled the car in and switched off the engine.

'I'm not here to prove anything. I'm not interested. What you've got inside you is a private hell and I can't help you with that. I don't want to add to it. I have no facts, no proof, no story to go with to anybody. All I've got is a guess but I know it is true because nothing else makes sense. The truth is that Monica was your daughter but Jim wasn't her father. Her father is the man that I'm driving you to see right now and his name is Danny LeRoy.'

'Oh, Christ,' said Mary Henekey and collapsed.

CHAPTER
TWENTY THREE

Milton did not move except to lift her head back from the dashboard and to lay it gently against his arm. He felt her pulse and then supported her chin until she recovered. He gave her his handkerchief to wipe away the sweat from her face.

They sat in silence for a little while and he got out his cigarettes, gave her one and lit it. Then he restarted the car and drove out into the traffic. Neither of them spoke and for the first quarter of an hour Mary Henekey sat slumped in her seat staring blindly ahead but then she fidgeted and brought up her handbag from the floor and searched through it to produce her vanity case. She repaired some of the ravages to her face and then settled back into her seat. She no longer looked at the road but at Milton and he drove steadily on, eating up the miles to the turnpike beyond which lay the gates to Mannering Park.

He drove in through the gates and pulled in at the little hut of the attendant who took the money for the car park. He helped her out and gave her another cigarette and then took her arm and led her to the beginning of the park, which was laid out in formal flower beds and neat little paths. They walked in silence towards the sports field and the tennis courts and the open expanses of grass where young mothers had brought their children to play ball and take a picnic lunch.

He allowed her to choose the direction and she selected the circular asphalt path that ran around the perimeter of the park. They walked slowly and in complete silence for a long time.

'I never had any luck with men.' Mary Henekey said suddenly.

'Maybe you didn't know enough of them.'

'I've known enough to know that very few of them ever face reality, not in the way that women have to face it every day of their lives. I suppose that's why men have their football and boxing matches. Women don't need second hand excitement, they have enough tension in their ordinary lives. It is what makes them seem timid.'

'Do you despise Jim?' Milton asked.

'No. It's not his fault that he isn't what I thought he was going to be. I was young and stupid and full of illusions and I lost them. I resented having to lose them as early as I did. It was less than a year after we married. I was seven months pregnant and pretty tired because I'd worked up until six months because we needed the money. He came back from work late, I was in bed and he woke me up to tell me that he'd lost his job. He told me that the owners of the shop were putting in another manager because he didn't have enough drive.'

'That could happen to anybody, we can't all be world beaters.'

'You can use words to soften anything. I was very young then, not twenty, and I suppose I just took it for granted that because he was a man and a few years older than me that he knew more, was more competent, better at handling the world. I don't think that I was a fool or more starry-eyed than most girls, but I did accept the usual myths. I didn't expect to live in luxury or for him to be some kind of Prince Charming but I did take it for granted that it was his department to take care of me.'

'Most women do. They go to work for special things, a new car or something like that, unless they've got a husband who's sick or an absolute bastard. You sound very normal to me. You were young and you were pregnant; you wanted to feel safe.'

'We had to get out of the flat because it went with the job. We had two months to get out, which was just about the time my baby was due and all the decorating and planning I'd done was for nothing. It doesn't sound much, people get turned out of their houses every day and men lose their jobs every day, hundreds of them. It's not like being ill or maimed, it's not a tragedy but you're right, I was very young and frightened. I did not know what to do, all I could think was how unfair it all was and that if I wrote or went to see the managing director he would see how unfair he was being. I suppose I got a bit hysterical about it because finally Jim told me that it wouldn't be any good writing to anybody because the real reason that they sacked him was because his books were in a muddle and he'd already been warned twice before. It was only because they knew that I was expecting a baby that they'd gone easy on him and given him another chance.'

Milton gave her another cigarette. 'Was Jim upset as well?'

'After I'd got the truth out of him he seemed to think that that was all there was to it. He said he was sorry and then he got into bed and went to sleep. I've never felt so lonely in my life as I did lying there with him sprawled next to me. I felt trapped, cheated. I looked at him lying there with his mouth open and I thought, My God, what is going to happen to me, what have I married? I was under twenty years old and I had discovered that the man I had married was stupid and a liar. That he was even incompetent at lying, incompetent at everything. He had unloaded his problems onto me and could sleep not knowing or caring whether I could or not, and I was carrying his child. I can't give you any idea of how I felt.'

'No,' said Milton, 'but I think I can guess. A feeling of betrayal is always shattering. But when you come against the iron when you are very young, it is always something special. It feels as though the sun has gone in for good.'

'That's it, exactly.'

'But everyone gets kicked in the teeth sooner or later. Anyone with a decent childhood takes it for granted that they are going to be a winner until the day it happens to them. The way you react to the knocks is supposed to show whether you've got character.'

'Is it? All I know is that I never felt the same way about him again. I stayed with him, mothered him I suppose. But I never respected him again, he was just there, like another child.'

'Why did you stay with him?'

'Where would I go? A woman with a small child doesn't get many offers. I suppose I was frightened of being on my own, more frightened of that than what I had. It would be different if I could live my life over but everyone says that, don't they?'

'Would you have left him for LeRoy?'

'He never asked me. We never even talked about it. He just took it for granted that I would have an abortion and when I refused he tried to talk me into it. The thing he felt guilty about was Jim thinking that the baby was his, he didn't feel guilty about an abortion. That's a very masculine attitude, isn't it?'

'How did you feel about LeRoy?'

'He was the only real man that I ever knew. I respected him, admired him even. He was stronger than me and at the time that I first met him I'd had enough of men who were weak. I was ready for someone like him. I was only twenty-six but for six years I had been taking all the responsibility. I had found a house, got Jim a job, tried to make sure he did it properly, brought up my daughter, worked myself and ran our home.'

'So you had your baby.'

'Yes, I had my Monica, she was a beautiful baby and a lovely girl; an exceptional girl by any standards. I was lucky to have her for the time that I did.'

'Did you still see LeRoy?'

'He gave me a thousand pounds when I had Monica but I didn't see him. He cultivated Jim and went out of his way to help him. He used to avoid him before. It was not that he felt guilty, he was bewildered, it was a situation he could not control, that he could not dictate. I hated him for quite a long time. When I was pregnant and could see that his position, his status, his bloody convenience meant more to him than me or his child, anything that I felt for him died. If I could have done something to hurt him then I would have done so but I couldn't, of course, I had no weapons. I did think of seeing his wife and letting her know. I saw her occasionally.'

'I've met her.'

'I detested her, she used to patronise me but she does that to everyone. She likes to live other people's lives for them at second hand and then thinks that they ought to be grateful. But I didn't go to see her, I didn't do anything and when Monica was born Jim was so proud of her. I've lived a lousy life.'

'It's most lives,' said Milton. 'A writer once said that any life seen from within is a series of defeats and he wasn't wrong.'

'Including yours?'

'Including mine. The way you felt about him when Monica was born, why did you have anything more to do with him?'

She sighed and looked out over the playing fields. 'Does anyone ever know exactly why they do anything? What I should have done was to move away. I wanted to but I didn't have a lot of energy at the time and Jim kept making objections and there was a money problem anyway. I couldn't just produce LeRoy's money as if it was a Christmas present. I thought it would be all right; it wasn't as if we were living next-door to each other: the houses on the other side of the golf course might as well be in another country. It seemed to work out all right: I never saw him, not to talk to, a glimpse now and then as he drove by in his car but nothing more.'

'How did it change?'

'It wasn't anything dramatic. Jim lost his job again. He made a mistake in some estimate that his firm put up and they lost a lot of money. It isn't that he's lazy but he is careless and he thinks he can rely on charm. If things are going well he relaxes, takes it for granted that things can run themselves. He never learns. LeRoy and Jim were both in the army, and when Danny became president of the British Legion, Jim was appointed to the committee and they saw quite a bit of each other. I didn't like that but there was nothing that I could do about it. Danny engineered it all, of course, but Jim wouldn't have seen that.'

'I suppose LeRoy felt in that way that he could be nearer his daughter.'

'He was getting older and he'd got everything he wanted, all the material things; perhaps he was bored with them.'

'They wouldn't be enough, not once he'd really matured. Things would have moved into perspective then.'

'You're just making excuses.'

'No,' said Milton, 'certainly not for him. He got his priorities wrong; a lot of people do, perhaps we all do at some time. But I am of his age group and I've never had a daughter. I regret that very much and I know how I would feel if I did have a daughter who believed her father was someone else.'

'Well, he got to thinking about his daughter about eleven years too late. But when Jim lost his job that last time and Danny knew all about it, he must have made it his business to find out, he got Jim a job. I don't know what strings he pulled but he was careful to find him a job that he really could do, it's called a stock controller but really . . .'

'Clever,' said Milton, 'to fix him up with a job he could hold down on his merits.'

'Calculating, but I suppose that is his kind of cleverness. He is very good at manipulating people.'

'Did he try to get back to square one with you once he'd found Jim a job?'

'Not right away; he was more subtle than that. He used to ask Jim how the children were getting on and send me his regards. When Monica was eleven she won a junior county race and it was reported in the local paper. That was when his wife called on me. I don't know what he told her, something about remembering me, I suppose, and Jim being unlucky. Anyway she called round in her Lady Bountiful role and went on about Monica and what marvellous opportunities there were for girls these days. What plans did I have, would I be able to send her to university, and all with that terrible smile of hers.'

'What did you do?'

'After I had got rid of her, I rang him up at his office and told him to stay out of my life and Monica's. He asked me to meet him.'

'And you did.' It was not a question.

'Yes, I did. I was no longer a silly little girl, waiting to be picked off the Christmas tree. I was glad to be able to say to his face all the things that I had been thinking about. He said that Monica was his daughter and that there were all sorts of things that he could do for her. He said I shouldn't stand in her way. He even came out with that one about blood being thicker than water.'

'Jesus!'

'He is a very self-centred man. Because he was good at making money he thought that he was something special. I told him that the sort of choice he was talking about could only be made once and that he had chosen before Monica was born. That her life had its foundations and that he had no right to destroy them.'

'And what did he say?'

'He didn't know what I was talking about. He was hurt and he got angry but when I told him he was wasting his time he tried to charm me. He rang me up afterwards but I wouldn't talk to him. Then I began to see him in odd places. If Monica was playing tennis or running somewhere, I would see him at the back of the crowd. Sometimes I would see him if I was out shopping, and he would be sort of hovering. Then he made things difficult by inviting Jim and me to dances and business functions. It was all very cunningly done because they were always vaguely connected with the British Legion or Jim's work. I kept making excues but, of course, Jim was very keen; he thought it meant that he was getting in with the right people. It was very difficult.'

'Did you go to any?'

'No, I'd made myself a promise about that. I always gave Jim an excuse and then I would ring up Danny and tell him to leave me alone. But he wouldn't, he took to giving Jim lifts home and coming in for coffee. I couldn't do anything about that.'

'Did you ever think of telling your husband?'

'I lay awake at night thinking about it. I didn't want anything to upset Monica and I knew that once I told Jim she would be sure to know. It would have been a relief to have told him, maybe I would have if he had been some other kind of man. But if he had been some other kind of man it would never have happened in the first place.'

'Yes,' said Milton. He looked across the park to the bank of small shrubs and plants that had been set out in representation of the town's coat of arms. The clarity of the cold sunlight was piercing. It was Milton's favourite season, the season of rich colouring, misty coolness and change; the hinge of the year in which he could feel both settlement and the movement of life to come.

'Have you any more cigarettes?'

Milton gave her one and produced his matches. 'When did you really meet him again?'

'I put him off for a long time; I wouldn't have anything to do with him. I told myself that I still hated him but I didn't, of course, I couldn't be bitter any more. I saw him as he was, a selfish, calculating man but there was something pathetic about him. He was bewildered because he couldn't understand why his weapons no longer worked, his money, charm, force of character, all his little manouevres. I told him that I wasn't interested in his money or in him. He had so many little tricks, so many carefully calculated arguments but none of them meant anything to me.'

'Did Monica know him?'

'She saw him.'

'She liked him?'

'She was flattered by him. He was always very interested in what she had to say, in what she was doing, in what she hoped to do. It is very flattering for a girl of her age to be taken seriously by a mature man. Particularly a man like Danny; he is very good at finding the right words, and he has style, it's very impressive. I know.'

'But you kept him at bay?'

'Oh, I handled him all right. I couldn't stop him seeing Monica casually, I didn't really want to; I just didn't want him to have any say, any control. He thought he could wear me down or bribe me but he couldn't, and then, of course, it all changed. He did not appear for weeks and then he telephoned me and said he had to see me urgently. I refused at first but he said it was a matter of life and death and I did meet him and he told me that he was going to die. It was in this park.'

She rose abruptly and stared into the middle distance. When Milton got up she walked away from the roses and they went together in silence, along the path and up by the little boating pool and then towards the sports ground where schoolboys were playing football.

'That must have been quite a moment,' Milton said eventually.

'I thought he was lying, some kind of cheap trick, but after a bit I knew it was true. It wasn't that he looked bad, but there was something about him, something about his eyes. A wariness, a kind of trapped look.'

'I know what you mean.' Milton looked away from her to

follow the flight of a late swallow.

'He told me that he had a lot of trouble with his stomach and he'd gone into a clinic in London. They had operated on him, an investigatory operation and afterwards they tried to fob him off but he insisted on knowing the truth. They told him in the end but it didn't do him much good.'

'They would have told his wife.'

'She wasn't there, she had gone to Switzerland. What they had found was that the growth in his stomach was malignant, they'd taken it out but the tests showed that it was growing again. There was nothing they could do, it was only a matter of months.'

'Poor devil!'

'Yes. He cried when he told me, and afterwards we drove out in his car to some wood up past the golf course and sat there for hours. He kept saying how sorry he was for the way he had treated me and for the things he had thrown away, for the waste of everything.'

'And he was frightened of dying.'

'It was more of a kind of bewilderment, a sort of rage at it all ending before he had done what he wanted to, against the triviality of it. He kept saying that the only important things in his life had been Monica and me.'

They were very close to the footballers now and Milton put his hand on her elbow to steer her away towards the deserted side of the sports ground.

'I wanted to get out of that car and run away, not to get away from him, poor devil, but so that I could be alone. But I couldn't and he was watching me, hanging on every word I said. I had to give him some kind of an answer. All I could think of was Monica, the effect it would have on her, the shock of finding out about the lies, that she was really someone else's daughter. I tried to imagine it happening to me. It would have undermined her whole life and I said no. I've been thinking about that ever since, about what I should have done.'

'You were right.'

'Was I, was I really? If I had told Monica the truth she would be alive today, unhappy maybe, but alive. I'm responsible for her death.'

'You're not. We all have to face up to the things we do,

mistakes included, that's all that anyone can do. No one on earth can accept the guilt for what someone else does, at any age or time. To think that is a kind of madness. If you had told Monica you would have destroyed your husband and Monica herself, in a different way. You had no choice but to prevent that. Maybe some other woman, less intelligent or wanting to get rid of a burden without bothering at its cost to other people. But you aren't that kind of woman, it's not the way you are. You are you.'

'I am me, the story of my life.'

'The story of anybody's life. Did you know it was LeRoy straight away?'

'No, I thought it was a maniac. I was in a state of shock and it came on top of everything else, the strain of the months with LeRoy when he used to ring me up all the time and having the feeling that he would suddenly appear. I went to pieces. I had been trying so hard to appear normal all that time and suddenly I could let it all go. The doctor gave me some pills and I slept for twenty-four hours. That was a very peculiar thing to have happened; they got worried. I suppose they thought I might have taken an overdose of something. But after that first shock, after the first day, I did begin to put things together. I thought it was peculiar that Danny had not tried to see me. And then when the police went on and on about who Monica knew and what sort of girl she was and would she have got into a car with a man she didn't know, well, I didn't have to work it out, I just knew. Monica had died and it was her real father who had killed her. In a strange way, knowing that, gave me a kind of peace. You saw me, didn't you?'

'You were in your garden.'

'And you thought I was odd. I could see it in your eyes, you thought I was very odd.'

'Not odd, but different, abstracted, as if none of it mattered. I thought that you knew who had killed Monica and that you were protecting him.'

'You're very perceptive, I knew you had sensed something. Who was it that you thought I was protecting?'

Into Milton's mind came the long face and soft brown eyes of Jim Henekey. 'I couldn't think of anyone. I didn't think it through to that extent; I just had the feeling of something being out of key.'

'And you've kept on from there.'

'I'm not a bloodhound. I'm not rated much as a detective. It was accidental, I live where I do and I wonder about things. When something doesn't fit it jars on me and it nags away at the back of my mind until I can find an explanation for it. It's always feelings that get the better of me. I've never been much good at manipulating facts.'

'And now you know.'

'Now I know.'

'I can't stop you stirring it all up again.'

'You're a remarkable woman; anyone else would have tried to swear me to secrecy or told me that she would deny it all if I ever repeated it.'

They had slowly reached the main gates of the park and they stood aside to let three young mothers go by with their small children.

'The nursing home is around the corner.' She gestured with her arm but she made no move to go through the gates.

'He's going to ask you to forgive him.'

'He's already done that, he wrote to me.'

'He wants to say it.' Milton moved nearer to the gates but she remained where she was.

'I can't see him.'

'He's screwed himself up to it, he can't stand the burden, he'll have to get rid of it one way or the other.'

'I can't carry his burden. I am finished with burdens and with lies. I don't care any more. Monica's dead and him—he's finished as well now. It's all finished, I just can't see him. He'll cry and—I don't want to hear him say it. I would never forget it if I had to hear him say it.'

'I'll take you back.'

'Leave me alone.' She jerked her arm away from him. 'I don't want any more talk. I want to be on my own. I want to be with my daughter. I don't want you to drive me. I'll get a taxi.'

He watched her walk away. Even with her head down she walked with a natural grace. He watched her walk all the way across the sports field until she was lost among the trees on the other side, and then he turned and made his own way through the gates of the park.

CHAPTER
TWENTY FOUR

The nursing home had once been someone's manor house, but now, with the addition of outbuildings and parking area, it had the look of all institutional buildings, but the curse was lifted a little by the dazzling display of rose trees that swept in from either side of the house. Their colours were better at a distance and as he approached the house he could see that the roses were overblown, waiting for the first of the autumn winds to shower the petals over the drive and lawns: their scent was sickeningly heavy.

There was no difficulty about seeing LeRoy. A motherly receptionist rang through on a house phone to check that he was not receiving treatment and was willing to receive a visitor, and then she told Milton the room number.

The corridor was uncarpeted but discreetly hushed with only the faintest trace of the aroma that he usually noticed in hospitals. The floors had been recently polished, the paintwork was very bright and the oaken doors were genuine. Everything was discreetly expensive.

LeRoy's room was at the end of the corridor and as he approached it the door opened and a nurse came out, young but not extremely young, she was the personification of bright efficiency and she flashed Milton a bright, professional smile.

'Mr LeRoy is all ready for you.'

Milton hesitated at the door before he tapped on it and went in. LeRoy was in a very high bed, propped into a sitting position by a support frame. The shoulders were still broad and the neck strong but the eyes that turned expectantly towards him were lacklustre, the mouth a little slack and there was a translucence on the skin. It was frightening that so formidable a man could be so altered by the touch of the first finger of death.

'I was expecting someone else.'

'I know, I'm sorry.'

'Mary sent you?'

'No.'

There was a chair on the far side of the bed, by the window and Milton pulled it closer to the bed.

'Why?'

'She did not want to come.'

'Who are you?'

'Milton, a policeman.'

Stupefaction came across the face and then the head dropped. The hands came up and then dropped away and something like a sob came out of the slack mouth.

'Don't be frightened.' Milton pulled the chair closer so that he was at the edge of the bed and could look up at the face and into the eyes. Eyes with the pupils so dilated that they were almost wholly black and reflected in each his own tiny image. The image of the interrogator, benign but insidious, seeking the human connection, the point of entry. And all that looked back were the unfathomable pools of darkness, filled with pain and bewilderment: the eyes of a dying animal.

'She told the police.'

'I already knew.'

'What will happen?'

'Nothing,' said Milton, 'nothing can happen now.' The eyes became unbearable and he looked away from the bed to the open window and outside to the massed late roses. There was something oppressive about their over-ripeness and he looked back to LeRoy again.

'I'm not here officially. The enquiry into Monica's death has ended.'

'Then why?'

'I know Mary, I know her family. I know you were expecting her and I thought someone should come to tell you that she will not see you.'

'I must see her.'

'No.'

'But why?'

'She couldn't bear it: she has enough burdens.'

'But I must—I want her—'

'To forgive you?'

'—to understand, I must make her understand.'

'Perhaps she does understand. She told no one about you, her husband, the police—nobody. I told her, because I had guessed, but there is no proof. There is nothing official about my being here. I came only because otherwise you would still be waiting or hoping that she would come tomorrow. She will never come, and I thought that it was better for you to know that.'

'I see.' Something happened to the man in the bed, the face was still bloodless but the jaw tightened and the head became more erect on those massive shoulders.

'It was the only thing to do.'

'You're not just a policeman are you? You're a detective.'

'I'm a detective sergeant.'

'And you guessed so you must be a good one. No one else has done that, I've seen the papers. It doesn't matter, nothing matters, except to be remembered as a—a— . . .'

'It's over.'

'I'm going to die.' It was a flat statement that hung in the still air of the room.

'I'm sorry.'

'You're sorry? Knowing what happened.'

'I don't know exactly what happened.'

'If there is ever a right time then this is it for me. I hope I can do it with a bit of dignity, it will be difficult if there is too much pain but the dying doesn't matter.'

'What about your wife?'

'She'll be all right, she'll get everything. It should have been different but it won't be now. Are you going back to Mary?'

'I don't know.'

'I came a long way. No, I thought I had come a long way, it was really a very little way. People thought I had everything, everything, that is, except children. Less successful men sometimes made a point about their children, telling me what fun they had with them. I suppose they were trying to show me that they had something that I hadn't. It was not true, Monica was my daughter. I never acknowledged her; I never did what I should have done. I took the soft option. I even enjoyed the secret knowledge of having a daughter that no one knew about. It's only in these last months that I've realised that I am a very unpleasant man.'

'But she never knew that she was your daughter.'

The voice became thin and hesitant. 'No, Mary refused to tell her. I've wanted to tell her, for years now, but Mary wouldn't—she—and then I had the pains. I knew what it was, I refused to believe it but I knew, really, inside I knew. I once had a partner who had exactly the same symptoms. I tried to ignore it, I was frightened of knowing what it was but it got worse, it got so bad that I couldn't hide it. I went to a specialist and made him tell me, the truth I mean, he didn't want to but he did. And I was shattered, I thought I could take it but I couldn't, everything lost its meaning, everything. Except Monica. I used to see her; for the past two or three years I would go anywhere to see her, past her school when they were leaving, on sports days, in the street, anywhere that I could. She was beautiful, a marvellous girl, everything anyone could wish for and she was my daughter and she did not know. It was agony. The pain I had was nothing to that.'

'I can understand that.'

'I wanted to do something. I told Mary that I was going to die. I wanted her to know me, I wanted her to have everything, I wanted . . .'

'But Mary said no.'

LeRoy wiped his eyes. 'She said I had made my decision all those years ago, that I had forced her to live a lie and that I could not ruin her life all over again. She said it wasn't fair to her or to Monica or Jim, that it would shatter all their lives to tell the truth now. I had to agree, I saw it as my just punishment. I promised to do nothing.'

'And you did?'

'Until that night. I thought I had accepted it until that night on the North Road when she was suddenly standing there, all in white, like a vision. I stopped the car, I had no thought of even talking to her, I just wanted to look, to admire. But, of course, she knew me and ran up to the car and opened the door, she thanked me for giving her a lift. I just nodded and drove on, she chatted about her club, her family, she was charming, so full of life. My God, I had never seen anything so beautiful in the whole of my life. I loved her, loved her as my daughter; I wanted to protect her, give her my name, everything I could, everything I had. All I wanted to do was to give. In no time at all I was past the turning that led to her road and she told me I had missed it. I said I would take her on the long road round and she said nothing. She must have begun to wonder. I couldn't find the words. I could not speak. At the common I pulled in, not really on the common, in the lay-by. I tried to speak but all that came out was her name and she tried to open the car door, she could not operate the safety catch because she was shaking, up against the door as far away from me as she could, looking at me with absolute disgust. I put my hand out to stop her from opening the door but my hand came down on her knee. She screamed. All I wanted to do was to stop her from screaming. To keep her quiet while I told her. My daughter.' His voice choked.

Milton sat rigidly in his chair. He looked at LeRoy slumped sideways on the pillows of the supporting frame. And then, you poor bastard, you took her out of the car and you laid her on the grass and then you tried to make it appear as though she had been violated. Because that part of your brain that made you such a bloody great success, that calculating manipulative part, was still working, still calculating the odds. And that is the true torture, that memory for which you can never obtain forgiveness.

The choking had subsided and the room was very quiet. LeRoy had turned his face away. Milton got up very carefully and replaced the chair. He crossed the room, opened the door and went through it into the corridor without looking back.

In the park the schoolboys were still intent on their game of football but most of the young women and children had departed. Men on their way home from work now walked the asphalted paths, armed with document cases and newspapers.

He walked through them until he reached the car park and then he took a long time unlocking his car. When, finally, he fired the engine he drove slowly from the car park into the mainstream of traffic. It became suddenly very important to avoid the direct route that would bring him once again to the North Road and the bus stop outside the tennis club at which Monica had waited. He turned off into an interlacing of back streets that led south of the railway line and forced him into a wide detour of the arterial road and into the centre of the industrial belt.

Streams of cars were coming out of the factory gates bringing the traffic to a walking pace. He pulled the car into the kerb outside a squalid looking public house and entered a bar crowded with heavy men wearing industrial overalls and donkey jackets. He pushed through the jostling, indifferent crowd and bought a whisky and then another; they brought a slight warmth to the ice within him and he bought some more. He went on buying them until he caught the eye of the landlord: he put his hand up to his face and felt the cold sweat that had collected across his forehead. He finished the drink he had and went out to his car.

He drove on and on, through the meanest of the streets, until he reached the giant cement works on the corner of the viaduct road which brought him again to the north of the railway and into familiar territory. The whisky had lost its heat and now only intensified his mood for abstraction. He drove with great care but as he neared his home he realised too late that the road he was on committed him to passing the Henekey house.

He took a deep breath and tightened his grip on the steering wheel but when he reached it it was just a heap of bricks like all the others. Houses do not show the conflicts within. He drove on to the final corner, swung wide across the crown of the road to line the car up with his drive-in but hit the accelerator too hard and had to brake savagely to stop the car from smashing into the garage door. He switched off the ignition and dropped the key. Something was wrong with his co-ordination, he fumbled badly in operating the door lever and his feet went the wrong way as he got out of the car.

His wife was already on the porch and he steadied himself against the car as she came out to him. He saw that she had been crying and he made a great effort to stand without swaying but when she reached him she smiled.

'It's wonderful, Arthur. A beautiful little girl.'